ERIC·M. HABERERN
PROPHECY

BOOK TWO OF *"THE HUNTER SERIES"*

ERIC M. HABERERN

Copyright

*****

Copyright © 2014 by Eric M. Haberern

Cover and internal design ©2014 by 2Faced Design

All rights reserved. No part of this book may be reproduced in any form or by any electronic or mechanical means including information storage and retrieval systems – except in the case of brief quotations in articles or reviews – without the permission in writing from its publisher, Eric M. Haberern.

All brand names and product names used in this book are trademarks, registered trademarks, or trade names of their respective holders. We are not associated with any product or vendor in this book.

ERIC M. HABERERN

Table Of Contents

*****

Dedication	07
Prologue	09
Chapter 1	11
Chapter 2	26
Chapter 3	33
Chapter 4	38
Chapter 5	51
Chapter 6	57
Chapter 7	71
Chapter 8	87
Chapter 9	97
Chapter 10	112
Chapter 11	120
Chapter 12	129
Chapter 13	141
Chapter 14	174
Chapter 15	186
Appendix	211
The Next Book	224
About The Author	226

ERIC M. HABERERN

Dedication

*****

There are so many people I can dedicate this book to, but I chose a few that truly deserved it. To my two sons Hayden and Ethan, thank you for letting me use your names and supplying me with the personalities for those characters. To my Mother, who no matter what I put her through as a child was always the first to tell me I was a good kid and would do great things. I hope I have made you proud. I love you, Mom.

C.A.

Don't EVER CHANGE FOR ANYONE......

Prologue

*****

Face-down in the rain, I realized slowly and painfully that the spell cast by the hooded figure had caught me completely off-guard. I groaned, pain ripping through me. It was intense. I was bleeding and felt sick and dizzy. Defeat taunted me and I closed my eyes, willing the thought of failure to go away. It was a paralyzing emotion and one that a hunter could not afford to have.

The minutes ticked agonizingly by, but I struggled somehow to my feet. Every muscle in my body ached and my wet clothes stuck to every sinew. The fog was dense. I tried to scan my surroundings for Lars, but the fog had swallowed him whole. I prayed he was safe. My brain felt as if it was swelling inside my skull and I swallowed hard – my mouth dry, a trail of blood dripping down my chin. I was lucky to still be alive. My assassin could have jumped down this rocky slope easily and finished me off; I could only imagine Lars was keeping him occupied.

My vision was blurred, I felt weak. The bone in my left arm jutted out at an unnatural angle and I leaned against the rock, one quick breath to prepare myself and then snapped the bone back into place. Waves of pain and dizziness swept over me and I gritted my teeth, I had to heal and heal quickly. It was starting to happen, the burning sensation of accelerated healing surged through me, but I doubted I would be healed in time. I had no choice but to face my demons unprepared and unfit.

Struggling back up the rocky slope, I clung to each rock, using every ounce of strength to carry my aching body forward. Finally, I pulled myself up, fog whirling around me. Despite the exertion, I felt cold, terribly cold, and fear gripped me, rendering me helpless. I tuned into my senses and shivered, the assassin was close. I scented the air, no fear, only malice. A glint of silver blade rose up out of the void, its curved blade the harbinger of death, and I staggered back, crying out as blood splattered across the rocky crag around me.

Chapter 1
Long Live The Queen

*****

We would be apart for almost two weeks. The realization was a depressing one. I could feel the tension rising within Catherine too as the demands of the Vampire Council began to weigh heavily on her again. I dreaded her leaving, it was as if the light went out of my world and I merely played at life in her absence. My green-eyed, brown-haired wife completed my being, was the essence of my soul, and without her, I felt lost. The summons to the Vampire Council came regularly now and each time on her return, she stayed locked away in our room. I had found it difficult to reach her emotionally. All these responsibilities to the Covenant of Light and Dark were just too much for one person to handle. Her father Vigo had been much older and more capable of handling this, I assumed. From my perspective, he had only lusted after the pain of others regardless of whether they were human or vampire. Catherine was not her father, thank goodness, though she found that she had to fill his shoes in this new world of ours.

I always tried to be supportive, suppressing my own resentment, but it was taxing on us. Fighting so hard to be with the one I loved did not always make me a good man. I resented the hours and minutes that we were separated. To deal with this loneliness, I had begun to train harder than I had ever done before, needing to work this frustration out of me. I was hardly alone, everyone else was supportive and especially Gloria, the werewolf leader of the Covenant of Light. She could somehow understand my mood changes, but I could also sense something else. She was glad when Catherine went away. I knew she could sense something different in me when Catherine was not around. Loneliness and a gaping void within emotionally perhaps.

Since the death of Vigo, the leader of the vampires, and the treaty with the Dark, the population of supernatural bad guys had diminished significantly. So Gloria, my friend Lars, and I practiced to stay sharp. I knew that the prophecy of balance between good and evil remained ever present and that a child had been predicted but this did not mean I could just sit and wait for fate to play a hand. I tensed and flexed my arm muscles, enjoying the sensation of blood pumping through my veins. Complacency would only tempt fate and there were still vampires and werewolves that had formed factions known as "The Children of Judas." Their purpose was to gain loyal followers in the name of Judas and to return evil to power.

I laid down my pen with a sigh, rubbing my eyes. They felt sore. My mother's diary of events was fascinating and filled with the intricacies of a story not truly revealed, and I have been using its empty pages to express my feelings. Since Vigo's death the Hunters' Journal had not summoned me. It was as if it had become dormant. I needed to know its secrets but, they were still closed to me. It was possible to see that the

PROPHECY

side of the Light had won the war between good and evil, but this was not a cut-and-dried conclusion. There were plenty who would like to fight still to change the outcome. I looked down at the journal, it was old paper and the binding was barely holding it together. In my 200 years as a hunter, this journal has served as a reminder of my past – and that of my parents. Writing in my mother's diary brings them closer to me somehow and I feel as if I glean more from the stories each time. The diary enhances what I know already, it enriches my memories and those from the past, but there were no new truths – as yet.

I shut the diary tight, holding it firmly in my battle-scarred hands. This book was one of the most precious things to me and I could not resist caressing the embossed letters that spell out my mother's name. As I locked the diary and the journal away, I shook off the memories and remnants of the boy within, and Paxton the hunter took me over once more. I burned with frustration. I needed to find someone to fight.

* * *

Several thousand miles away across the North Atlantic, a fleet of cars, one carrying Catherine, converged on what was once a U.S. embassy, now used for diplomatic concerns of a supernatural nature. Catherine climbed out of the car, remembering what Paris had looked like before the war. She couldn't believe that it had been over 150 years since the last time she had set foot on this soil.

Surely it was only yesterday? How could life go by so quickly? The words hung in her mind for a moment and she tried to not let them go. Not because of the joy that the memories brought her but the pain that tainted the air that she breathed. She remembered all those who had died. "Human life is so fragile," Catherine whispered, noting just how much Paris had changed. Governments no longer did business directly with other governments and all communications and decisions were made through a centralized organization called the PHLC (the Preservation of Human Life Corporation).

After World War III, countries stopped making alliances and became their own sovereign entity. The PHLC came to power after the world's population dipped from 7 billion to 3.5 billion people. This organization, made up of so many different factions, formed a monopoly. The monopoly was allowed to exist because they had created drugs that could cure many of the diseases, and were able to speed up recovery time after surgery, slowing aging in the process.

These cures were all made possible by vampire doctors with the view that it made sense to preserve their food supply and possibly the next generation of vampires. The PHLC was a global powerhouse, the likes of which had never existed before. Catherine was the heiress to this empire. She had never known for sure what her father did other than try to find ways to torment and destroy humans. The distinctly cruel edge to him was not news but the way he approached it with business acumen was. She hadn't realized even after 500 years that he was not just trying to preserve the old ways, but to find ways to capitalize on capitalism itself. Catherine had never asked but knew it was her duty to carry on where the company left off although it pulled at her heartstrings.

PROPHECY

Escorted from the car and through the front doors, Catherine was guided down the hallway. The rooms on each side of the corridor were swathed in darkness. The head of security flanked her side, his face chiseled, like a mask.

"Why are the offices here all vacant?" she asked.

He glanced quickly in her direction, saying, "I do not know, nor would I be told why." His voice was firm and did not invite a response.

Catherine looked at all of the guards dressed in black, all sheep-like marching down the corridors in unison. They were protecting her and yet even with their enormous physiques, she knew she could kill them all if she wanted to. She envisioned transforming into her vampire form and biting down hard on fragile skin and bone. Maybe let a few run to increase the levels of adrenaline so that their blood tasted better. She continued to think about it as she walked, wondering about the differences between vampire blood and werewolf blood. She could feel the urge to feed sweeping up over her; her eyes became slightly glazed with the forthcoming transformation and the hunger made her stomach growl. She could imagine her father's face telling her to let go. It was at that moment she stopped walking, closed her eyes, quelling the blood lust, and turned away from the security detail, walking into one of the empty rooms.

"Stay back," she warned them. Ever since her father's demise, and more of late, she could feel the urge to be evil growing inside. It was a hunger like she had never known. She wondered if she was ill and a sickness was raging through her veins. Catherine knew she had to get a grip before she did something that she would regret.

The evil that lurked inside of her surged up even when she was with those that she cared about. At times the power consumed her so much that even when around Paxton she would long to attack him and to taste his blood. She had never told him this but tried her best to subdue the urges, terrified that she might lose control; this was mingled with disgust for her potential actions. She loved him so much and she could never let her heritage, and this seed of death within her, grow and consume all that she was.

Blood lust calmed and under control, she rejoined the security detail, and in silence they took an elevator up several floors to a very large meeting room. There, as she entered, sat the Vampire Council. Ominous faces. As CEO of the company they had established after War World III, she was the head vampire but they ran the business. She was the 13th vote and she could bring to the table new proposals, but it was more of a status position that even Catherine didn't want. Now, with her father dead and the council in full control of the Covenant of Dark, she had to attend all the important meetings face to face and this meant traveling to a variety of locations. In her lifetime she had only seen the council three times within the previous 500 years and now, three times so far in the last six months since her father's demise.

Catherine looked around the room and registered the 12 other council members. They seemed random by physique, looks, and gender. There were all different races. The only thing they all had in common was their

PROPHECY

love of money and power, and that they lived off human blood. The one requisite to be on the council was that they all had to be purebloods. Never would a half-breed or even a werewolf be a part of this elected board; this would not change in the coming millenniums.

They all stood as she walked into the room. Respect mingled with dislike greeted her. She was partially responsible for her own father's fate and that she shared her bed with the hunter known as Paxton Holt was unthinkable. They overlooked this for several small reasons. Her ability to walk in daylight as the only vampire who could do so, and that she was a direct descendant of Judas himself. There was also the small consideration that she was the most powerful of them all with the backing of the Covenant of Light.

Catherine took her seat and the others followed. She didn't know why these meetings put her on edge but they did. They seemed pointless, the meeting agenda irrelevant, and as the speaker droned on, she sat back and daydreamed about Paxton. The night before her departure, he had held her in his arms, their bodies entangled, woven together as their skin burned a trail from top to bottom. Even with immortality and his superhuman healing, Paxton had scars. This never stopped Catherine from running her hands over them. She explored them just as much as she explored other parts of his rippling body.

She would take her fingers and, moving up from his sculpted stomach, run her hands up over his rippling abdominal muscles. She would sense each one as she made her way up to his face where she placed a finger over his lips if he attempted to talk. It was then that she used her strength, and slipped deftly on top of him, holding him firmly between her thighs knowing how it excited him.

"Have your men found the location of the vampires that declared war against the treaty between the Covenants of Light and Dark?" The voice was impatient and broke into her reverie. Catherine felt the memory fragment as she brought her attention back to the room.

"We are afraid that if this is not dealt with soon we may see a backlash and repercussions from them." The voice came from Joakim Fredrik of Sweden – the Supreme Chancellor. Joakim had to be taken seriously. He was a very powerful vampire. He did not take pride in human suffering as Vigo had, but enjoyed the finer things that came with power and wealth.

Another voice in the room rang out, this time it was Baldassare Vega of Italy. He saw an opportunity to decry the slaughter of vampires regardless of whether they were committing crimes. He looked at the council and said, "Savages…who would have thought that we would seek harm on our own kind? This makes us no better than the humans we feed on."

Heads in the room nodded in agreement. The youngest female vampire on the council was the German Priscilla Rehborn. She looked young and vibrant, but the prettiness belied 600 years of war lust, trying to find ways that would benefit her from the death and carnage. She would support whichever cause or directive kept her alive and benefited her the most. Pricilla looked around the room and knew that most, if not all, of the

PROPHECY

other council members shared her feelings so she showed no reservations about speaking her mind.

She looked at the group and said, "Members of the Council, we have bled for each other over the centuries, and we lived to support Vigo even during the dark ages, but he is gone and the old ways died with him. We have been thrust into a new world, one filled with endless possibilities. Let's not forget this, but let's also not dwell on the past. We have a chance now to take this covenant in a direction that will preserve our species and increase our wealth for several millenniums."

Josiah Black, who was one of the longest-serving members, spoke out, his voice outraged. "Have we all gone mad? This is complete chaos. We have deviated so far from what our father had meant for us, may Judas have mercy on us all."

Priscilla spoke up again, her voice deep and laced with sarcasm. "Judas, Judas, Judas. That is all you ever speak. Where has he been all these years? Who watched out for us when we were slaughtered by hunters and destroyed by our own kind? We have become no better than the humans we feed on. You show me where he is and that he can give a damn about us and I will start giving a damn about him."

Several in the room lowered their heads, muttering the name of Judas for forgiveness. She just sat back and shook her head.

Joakim slammed his hand down hard on the table as his eyes turned red and his teeth bared. "I insist we have order!" he hissed in a very snake-like voice.

Catherine quickly composed herself, sitting up straight in her chair, her voice lowering in an authoritative manner. "Our scouts have found two small factions, but they keep moving. We think these groups are the main leaders of the movement. It seems as if either humans or werewolves were aiding them since they are being moved during the day. Their overall numbers have grown, however."

She paused, looking along the line of council members. "We have estimated them to be in the thousands at the moment but that number could be greater. We think if we can anticipate their next location, we can attack the leaders of this organization and either crush the order completely or at least cripple it until we can get more intel on additional locations and overpower the remaining forces."

"Catherine, why don't you send out your dog?" Zackariah Corbin – the New Zealand representative – sneered at her. "It is his job to hunt out and kill supernatural beings is it not?"

Catherine narrowed her eyes in warning. "Yes, but be aware that he is not my dog." She could feel her hands start to shake in sudden anger at her fellow council member's audacity. "I will meet with him and the Covenant of Light on my way back and formulate a strategy of attack. Trust me, members of this council, Supreme Chancellor, we will find the leaders of this group and put them out of their misery."

The council voted quickly and then moved onto the next subject. Catherine cooled her anger and once again drifted in and out of her fantasy, just counting down the days until she saw Paxton again. As she sat quietly, voices droning distantly around her, she knew such an ache inside, like a gnawing hunger. She lusted for his love and the heat of their two bodies pressed together.

* * *

At the same moment, in a concealed room protecting his opponent from the harmful rays of sunlight, Paxton was dueling with Lars. Lars had spent the last two centuries teaching Paxton the art of the sword. Lars knew he could never fill the shoes of Clay, the werewolf who had been Paxton's first teacher, but he did his best to mentor Paxton as much as he could. He felt that he owed this to him. He felt like a brother looking out for his younger sibling. Plus, it was Paxton and the prophecy that had brought about the destruction of Vigo, the vampire that killed his father.

Lars thought about the death of Vigo with great joy. He had resurrected his relationship with his brother Virgil and over time, Lars had softened, opening up and becoming someone that Paxton would trust implicitly. Lars knew that to be held in such regard by Paxton was an honor. He was an integral part of the close-knit family that surrounded Paxton and this only included Gloria, Catherine, and Hayden.

Lars had drifted from the battle and suddenly snapped back into gear as Paxton moved forward, the light glinting off the sharpened blade. Lars concentrated. Paxton did not like to use dummy weapons when sparring. There was no level of danger and the natural instincts to survive would never kick in. As Paxton swung his sword past Lars, the blade sliced a small piece of his long, blond hair, causing Lars to jump hurriedly to the side. His concentration suddenly pulsed. It was Paxton and he would never intentionally try to kill him, but if he made it too easy, he just might come close to wounding him.

They had played this game many times before. Paxton had beaten him only a couple of times. Lars was in fact considered the best sword fighter. In the centuries he had been alive, no one, not even Paxton, had ever truly had Lars in danger. Lars had hoped that if one day he was to die, it would be at the hands of someone who had the ability to out-duel him. That was the honorable death. A warrior needed to die by the blade. It was natural skill, along with practice, that had made him so good. He could learn the other person's weakness within minutes. It was at this time that his opponents would assume they had him where they wanted him, but instead, they experienced the intense pain of a sword slicing through the heart. Lars didn't play around when he fought for real. He was all business.

Lars became an extension of his weapon. The sword was one with him, and he made the blade dance through the air. It pirouetted like a ballerina until it struck like a cobra. Lars knew Paxton respected his ability. His dedication to his art was amazing. He was a Van Gogh with a blade, a Mozart with his moves. The combination made him one of the deadliest fighters on the planet.

Lars knew what Paxton would do. He had taught him everything the four great masters had imbued within him. They had spent nearly two centuries fighting together. The sparring could go on for days without stopping for food, water, blood, or even sleep. A sudden move from Paxton had Lars follow up quickly

PROPHECY

with a cross formation, just barely missing Paxton's face. Paxton was sparring in a different way, Lars realized. He was letting him win. Mistakes were creeping into his game. Lars narrowed his eyes, something was wrong. Paxton was lowering his guard between strikes using his enhanced speed as well as one of his mastered fighting styles called Senduci. It was a very old technique and made the person look weak, but its entire point was to strike hard and fast and to finish the opponent. Paxton had never attempted it before but Lars was sure he was about to try.

His student, once a skinny teenager with unruly brown curls, was developing, growing in confidence, willing to embrace the new and the old ways. Paxton had always wanted to utilize magic with his fighting style, but it had been too volatile. Lars knew that this time, Paxton was prepared to see whether would work. He took a deep breath, preparing his muscles for the onslaught to come.

As their blades met each other at each crossing point, sparks flew. The blades were made of a metal compound and balanced to perfection. Each strike made was met with a perfect defense. Lars took to the air. Flipping around like a gymnast, Paxton followed. Their strikes were met upside down and right side up, but each with a block. Lars sensed the moment Paxton spun into action. While flipping in the air, Lars noted in disbelief that Paxton had closed his eyes, he was lost in the moment but in doing so, he lost one of his senses. Lars smiled; he was going to enjoy teaching Paxton a lesson. Lars went in as they both met in the air, but right before his blade met skin, Paxton vanished. Lars in that very second was dumbfounded but continued his flip, twisting in midair, landing on his feet, the sword at his waist. Paxton reappeared with his sword raised and his blade inches from Lars' face. An unmistakable look of joy and satisfaction etched across his face.

Lars couldn't believe it. He had been bested by Paxton, who made the smallest move and sliced into Lars' cheek, knowing it would heal within seconds but sting his victory into the face of his friend. The mark wouldn't last but the way it was accomplished would resonate with both of them for a long time. Lars had always known if anyone had a chance to beat him it would be Paxton. Lars, with narrowed eyes and shaking his head, bowed in respect and walked over to his friend, placing an arm around his shoulders. "Paxton, my friend, that was one sweet move. I knew you had to do something different if you were ever going to win that match."

Lars touched his cheek as the skin puckered and began to heal. "Unbelievable." Lars laughed. Paxton took it as a genuine complement as Lars rarely gave anything away.

"I am glad you are on our side. I wouldn't want to face you as the enemy," Lars admitted, laughing.

"Thank you, Lars, coming from an old man that means a lot."

Lars dropped his sword and tackled Paxton to the ground as they finished with both of them wrestling on the floor, their laughter ringing around the length of the practice hall.

Ethan and Gloria watched silently. Ethan was somewhat new to Safe Haven. He was a pureblood vampire still considered to be in his teen years. He had been found in the jungles of Africa, hungry and dying. Gloria and the Covenant of Light had saved him and he had spent the last five years learning to control his hunger and deal with the ordeals of training. Ethan admired Paxton. They had a bond – a connection. As Lars was guiding Paxton, so Paxton extended the hand of knowledge to his new friend.

Gloria beckoned to Paxton and Lars. "We have Catherine on the screen. She has received a direct order from the 'powers that be' regarding those rogue vampires." Gloria scrutinized Paxton's face. His features remained unchanged, perhaps a little more relaxed. She wondered what he was thinking. Was he glad of the chance to fight again? She watched as Lars and Paxton made their way towards them, noting that Paxton had learned to hide his emotions well; it would serve him well in battle but she suddenly felt excluded. Was Paxton developing beyond their reach?

Chapter 2
Africa

*****

It was impossible to not feel claustrophobic, I realized. There was very little air in this confined space. Every single vibration from the plane reverberated through me. I knew I wasn't the only one experiencing a sense of agitation.

It was Ethan's first mission with us. I could tell that he too felt a little closed in. Memories of his time on a plane where he had been kidnapped and taken from the African jungle would be flooding back, I knew. He had been found naked and ravenous, feeding off anything that came within 30 feet of him. Those sorts of thoughts would not be a comfort to him and I could sense his inner angst. Lars, on the other hand, had his sword holstered in his lap as he leaned up against it, sleeping like a baby. I shook my head enviously, then turned my attention back to Ethan as he struggled openly to change his mind-set to something more positive before the beast that was within him came back.

As much as Ethan was struggling, I was able to remove any stray thoughts at will. It was a case of looking deep within and letting no thoughts intrude. Instead, I welcomed the sensation of pure silence. Intense practice had enabled me to settle at will and I was glad for that now. I leaned back, the warmth of the seat comforting against my back and supporting my large frame. As much as I could empty my mind, I could also focus with great clarity and the image of Catherine came into my mind. Only two days previously she had contacted me at Safe Haven and had confirmed the new location of the leaders of the Children of Judas. They were just inside the Congo in a place called Quesso. Protected by deep forests, humans, or werewolves, they would be a hard target to track down. Even the terrain was daunting, but then I relished a challenge.

The report provided by the council had not been made clear but the tone of the order had been. Catherine was in an impossible situation. She was businesslike and professional but when we reconnected, her gaze would soften and I could see the intensity of her love; for a while she could leave all the nonsense of the council behind. That she was missing me was a double-edged sword. My own love swelled within me while my heart felt as if it were being squeezed because she was no longer by my side. I knew that Catherine had doubted Gloria's wisdom when it was announced that Ethan would be traveling with us but she had acquiesced. Ethan was still new – only just over 100 years as a vampire and reconditioned at Safe Haven for just five years. I resisted a wry smile at the length of a suitable apprenticeship.

My mind drifted lazily back to the meeting. Gloria had asked a lot of questions but she was right to push for answers. We needed to know if we had clearance to fly in or if we would have to find a way around their military perimeter.

Since War World III, no one trusted flying into a country uninvited. Catherine knew that the African president would not just open his doors to a Canadian plane. Catherine had been very clear in her response: "You will have your clearance, but your window will be small. As soon as you cross into their airspace, you will have just 24 hours to complete your mission. If you are not out of Africa by then, they will utilize every weapon in their arsenal to shoot you down. They do not take prisoners and we cannot reveal who or what we are. So you must not fail."

I could hear the worried tone of her voice even now but gradually other voices filtered through.

"Unidentified aircraft, please advise your business, over."

The pilot responded, "African Command Central, we have clearance from the President himself and are permitted immunity for 24 hours. Clearance code 11 Alpha Tango 378 Foxtrot 053, over."

There was a pause that seemed to last for eternity. I held my breath while a decision was made. To one side of me, I noted Ethan waking up Lars who had been sound asleep. As Ethan unstrapped himself and went to shake his shoulder, Lars grabbed his hand. "Don't touch me, boy. I am up. Remember, always one eye open at all times."

"You are cleared to utilize the nearest airstrip for landing and refueling," the command told our pilot. "You have 24 hours. When that time elapses and if you have not left this country, we will be forced to declare you prisoners and you will be executed by ways of Order 86."

PROPHECY

I raised an eyebrow. Friendly bunch, but I had no doubt that they meant every word.

War World III had started in 2045 over control of the oil refineries in the Middle East. The war had lasted for 22 long years. It was in November 2067 that Order 86 was instituted; it stated that each country that had declared itself a sovereign nation would not permit anyone to leave or to flee to another country. Should this rule be disobeyed, the country in question had the right to kill those who entered and there would be no retaliation. I knew of only one group that was issued immunity from Order 86 and this was the PHLC. They were not affiliated with any one government. Since the trade between countries had stopped, the PHLC had become the middleman. By 2080, the PHLC controlled 97% of all trading between countries. There was still the black market that made up about 3% of the trade but much of that was ammunition and weapons. The PHLC dealt in everything from apples to zippers.

The pilot glanced in my direction. He looked concerned and I knew he was thinking that this was really a one-way mission. "I will be at this latitude and longitude. As you heard, you have just 24 hours to get in and get out. Good luck."

We nodded our heads in unison. We knew that fate was against us. It wasn't just the problem of the vampires and werewolves but the forthcoming sun too. Night was invading the country. We had timed it just right but we really only had 12 hours of darkness to get the job done. The back of the cargo hold only had light from within.

Lars and Ethan suited up. They both wore full-black leather garb; in their drop packs they had a helmet that kept out the UV rays. This would protect them if we had to work during the day. I hoped that the mission would be easier than anticipated and that the element of surprise was still with us. This should almost certainly guarantee us victory.

I looked at Lars and Ethan as the back opened. The sun had fully set and all we could see was the black of night. The wind swirled in the plane. The heat was intense. I knew it was now or never. I nodded at my companions and we set our watches for 23 hours, just in case we were separated. There was an hour to spare if things went really wrong.

Lars jumped first. Ethan hesitated and I knew he had to face this fear.

"Push it out of your mind," I ordered. "You control it, it does not control you."

Ethan looked helplessly at me. Fear had him gripped like a vise, the reality of the drop freezing him into inaction. With undisguised frustration, I kicked out at Ethan and knocked him out of the door, watching as he plummeted like a stone before pulling the handle of his chute. I allowed a small smile, problem solved.

The moon looked incredibly full, the silver shafts of light cascaded across the expanse lighting up the skyline. I knew once we dropped beneath the canopy of trees, the light would be diminished. The darkness didn't scare me but I couldn't help but wonder what lurked below us sheltering in the undergrowth. The darkness was ideal camouflage for werewolves who would be at home in this habitat.

PROPHECY

I mentally calculated the weapons that I had strapped to me. Guns, swords, ammo, and strapped to my leg, the kill instrument. No one ever understood the connection I had with it. As my fingers touched it, I could feel my heart beating steadily, pulsing within as the connection was made. The kill instrument was a part of me.

I pulled the handle of my chute as I caught up with Lars and Ethan. Still a hundred feet in the air from the top of the canopy, Lars released his parachute and fell the rest of the way. I saw Ethan's fear escalate and he looked at me in disbelief. I shook my head and watched Lars twist in the air, narrowing his body in the way a seamstress would do with a piece of thread ready to push through a needle. He passed through the top layer of the trees uncontested and then bat-like spread his arms, grabbing a branch and swinging himself down level by level until he was safely on the ground.

Ethan and I followed safely and landed in a less ceremonious way. Once free from the chute, I pulled out my com-link, flipping it open with both hands to call base. The screen lit up as I did so. "Base – do you read me? This is Party of Three. We are safely on the ground, over."

A familiar voice rang over the com-link, Gastin. "It's good to hear your voice, stranger. I am sending over the coordinates, map, and location to you now."

My com-link blinked as the information arrived.

"The system will blink as you get closer to your target. Also, note that these new com- links have body heat tracers. They show up as a green dot."

"I have one."

"It is your heat signature. Lars and Ethan do not have one for obvious reasons. It can be useful but don't forget to rely on your instinct, which is the best warning system you will have. Good luck, my friend."

The system went quiet and I drew in a deep breath. We were here, ready to go, and we had limited time, but I needed a moment to let my movements become instinctive. Paxton the hunter had to emerge. I checked the map and noted the direction; we had to be stealthy and cautious. I did not for one moment believe that it would be entirely easy to fulfill this mission and I didn't want to lose anyone else from my team.

It was time to go. I looked at Ethan and Lars and nodded. A quick weapons check and we were off, slipping through the blackness of the forest towards an unsuspecting enemy.

Chapter 3
The Stranger

*****

Voices could be heard in the distance and we slowed down instinctively. The structure in front of us seemed fragile but I had a feeling that it was much more than it appeared to be. It had to be. My senses were tingling. An abandoned room lay directly ahead of us, and from my sideways position, I could see inside, noting a table and chairs and a small wood-burning stove. There was a small bed in the far corner and then a door that appeared to lead back outside the shack.

I glanced around us nervously; my heart was beating rapidly beneath my ribs. The com-link blinked to alert me to the way and I moved towards the entrance, the others following me. New information revealed that the doorway led to an elevator shaft, some 40 feet below ground. We walked quietly into a room that contained long outdated systems and spent a few moments checking the equipment. It was as if the room had been hurriedly thrown together. I wondered if this was the case. Satisfied that there was nothing of interest, I fought my rising sense of danger and we stepped into the elevator, which juddered its way down to the underground location.

There was no one around. I had half-expected a welcoming party but there was no indication that anyone was here. We emerged silently, padding softly down the cement-floored corridor towards one of the bunkers. Even with the equipment being so dated, it was far beyond what the governments had been using during War World III. The room set-up had possibly been established by the government of Africa for its regime or it could have been set up by the vampires themselves to protect their numbers during the war.

There were food supplies; I wondered if this was used to feed humans who may have been kept here and who were potentially a living food cupboard. Regardless of who had built it and why, it was currently occupied. This bunker did not house just one single room. It spread down several corridors. Down on the right-hand side was a kitchen that was well-stocked with food and a freezer and then down on the left, there was a command room. I could see from my vantage point that this room had maps of the world with points designated on it. There was also a giant screen, which at the end of the 21st century had been used as the primary communication for continent-to-continent and country-to-country messages. This was widespread because travel had become so expensive due to rocketing gas prices.

When War World III ended, traveling out of your own country was next to impossible because of Order 86. Many people feared that they would be marked as enemies of the state and killed, so they braved it and attempted to flee. The governments had no choice but to kill any of them that weren't successful. This was clear-cut genocide, but no one did anything about it since it was technically the law. Thousands upon thousands in countries all over the world died by firing squad, bombs, or drowning. Humanity had taken a nosedive from equality back to slavery and butchery was rife.

War was crazy. Nations that once shared in each other's prosperity, love of freedom, and passion for sports had turned their backs on each other. The door was well and truly shut and the key thrown away. With travel halted, the giant com-links allowed for meetings on diplomacy to continue, but the war and the number of casualties soured any potential resolution and so order 86 was kept in place. Peace could have been reached but no faction trusted any other. The only thing that every nation could agree upon was Order 86.

The command center had a table in the center of the room. I could see several men surrounding this table now, not unlike those that would have patrolled the unit on January 7, 2067, when the war had finally ended. Unlike that day, these men were not celebrating an end to a historic time in human history. They were planning to make history – that of the supernatural kind. A new war was beginning, one that would not see human vs. human but monster vs. monster. Powerful beings, able to withstand the sands of time, who would rise up against each other. Somewhere in all of this murderous mayhem and pure chaos would be me.

These supernatural beings were not just of any group. They were some of the most powerful of an era past, led by General Lark. He was one of Vigo's top three, and the survivor now that Voss and Otho were dead. He had two things they didn't, a plan and his head. He had another something too, a supporter, someone very powerful who even General Lark didn't know in person but who had perpetrated this new rebellion. Known only as the hooded figure, he was thought to have helped finance the rebellion. There were just a few loose ends to be eliminated before they could proceed.

Voices exploded like fireworks, erratic bickering sounds rose to a crescendo, ending abruptly as the giant screen crackled and an image appeared. Peeking around the corner, I was surprised as the chemicals from the 150-year-old screen warmed up, fuzzy at first, but then with greater clarity as the picture emerged. I breathed in sharply. Clearly visible on the screen was the hooded figure, concealed completely apart from glowing red eyes. I felt a tremor of anticipation, as the eyes seemed to rip into my soul.

"Have you assembled your army, General Lark?"

"Yes. We are ready."

"The camp is under threat. You have intruders who have located you and who may even now be inside. They are very powerful and are led by Paxton Holt. Our informant has provided this information and has activated a beacon that will display on your com-link. Kill the vampires and bring us the hunter."

From my vantage point, I could see General Lark's eyes turn blood-red as anger surged through him and his fangs extended from the roof of his mouth. This outward show of aggression was not false; it fired the energy and determination for victory. I knew the general had an intense hatred of me and here I was cowering in the shadows, when my instinct was to run in there and annihilate them all.

PROPHECY

"You will get him alive," the General vowed, shouting at his closest comrades, but I knew that if I was captured, there would be very little left by the time they had finished with me.

The screen went dark as the wiring and transistors emitted a low buzzing sound and the screen cooled down. My heart was beating erratically. Once he had enabled the com-link, he would be able to see just where I was. The werewolves were on standby, chomping at the bit desperate to get to me. I could smell their rising scent as frustration and blood lust surged to the surface. He gave the order, but the plan had been conceived long before we had infiltrated their camp. He knew his master had a plan and had prophesied this journey – we were bait. The 12 men inside no longer looked like men, they had changed. They had allowed their true nature to take hold of them. Each one hid in the shadows just waiting. Outside the werewolves had their orders and then the call over the com-link crackled.

"Drive them into the house, then surround it. Don't let them escape. Do not enter unless I tell you so."

The werewolves took their positions. This was a calculated ambush. They wanted my head on a platter – an offering to the hooded figure. I had to make sure they didn't achieve their end game. The Covenant of Light had informed us we would only have to deal with maybe four to eight rebels; I started to wonder if we had been sold out and whether there was an informant in our midst. That thought scared me more than the mob of blood-lusting vampires and werewolves.

Chapter 4
Ambush

*****

We had slipped quietly away – the elevator noiselessly moving us out of immediate danger. We spread out into the night, choosing our cover carefully. I took up a position at the right, Lars took up the left and Ethan remained at the back using his amazing vision to detect trouble ahead. He kept his eyes firmly focused. With his vision firmly locked, he was now vulnerable to close attacks. His only defense was his sense of smell, which he had accessed many times during fights and sparring with Paxton, Lars, Gloria, and mostly with Giovanni.

Giovanni had lived at Safe Haven for over 300 years. He was a half-breed werewolf, but he fought and carried himself as a full-blood. He had fought hard and ascended up the ranks to become the personal detail to Gloria. Wherever she went, he went. If a silver bullet was coming for her, Giovanni was the one that would take it, even if it meant certain death.

Gloria had put faith in him when no one else had. He was lost when Gloria found him feeding off of animals in her territories. She found him just around the time she had lost a few good soldiers and needed more able bodies. She offered him refuge and good meat to eat. Giovanni was no alpha by any stretch of the imagination, but he had worked so hard for the last 200 years that he had earned his spot and had held it for 100 years. Ethan had certainly learned a lot from Giovanni. His blind dedication was unparalleled. He had stepped in with both feet and had promised to give his life for Gloria no matter what. It took him a long time to fit in, but he never made waves. He lost more matches while training than he won. He was looked at as just a poor half-breed, but it never stopped him from striving forward and seeking approval from us. Because of his attitude over the last 100 years, he had rightly gained the respect of the inhabitants of Safe Haven, winning more matches subsequently than he had lost.

Ethan was beckoning to me. His keen eyesight had detected some movement from around the shack and two men, barely detectable in black suits, walking towards the door. I nodded at Lars and he moved in. Sword drawn, he moved forward low, silent and prepared. Something was wrong though; I could sense it but couldn't define it. I signed Lars to stay where he was. I couldn't see any actual danger; Lars looked confused but still this nagging feeling inside of me persisted. We waited. I tuned into every sense I possessed, but I couldn't detect more. Was this just my fear of losing a member of my team? Reluctantly, I signaled Lars in and he sprung up from the ground, his alignment in a perfect position for attack.

Howling filled the air. It came from all directions. I could sense the blood lust. We were surrounded. Red eyes narrowed and appeared in their masses from out of the darkness. They smoldered with hatred and an intense thirst for our blood. I grabbed the kill instrument instinctively and noticed it was glowing bright silver. Lars ran back and flanked my position on the side while we waited for the werewolves to rush in at us. We had a battle on our hands.

I looked back for Ethan. He was gone. I prayed he had hidden when he had seen the danger but I had a sick feeling in the pit of my stomach that he had been taken prisoner or worse, was dead.

"Get the feeling we were given wrong information?" Lars queried.

"Something like that," I agreed.

These were not just a few rogue vampires and werewolves that we were facing, this was a whole army. We were now in the middle of a battle where survival seemed impossible.

"Just tell me how many of them I get to kill." Lars was starting to change. His teeth were baring and his already piercing blue eyes had turned to an ultra-blue. Vampire eyes were always red but Lars was different, it was disconcerting but he liked being different.

"Feel free to kill as many as you want," I replied flippantly, "just leave me the odd one or two to clear up." I tried to smile but my mouth was dry and my lips were sticking to my teeth.

Werewolves were growing ever closer. They hissed and growled, baring their teeth while drool flowed from their mouths. They were hungry. They slowly moved in towards us. I needed to come up with a plan, but had no idea what. It seemed as if this could be the end.

***

Ethan was now paralyzed to the spot. He had managed to move further out of sight, crawling on his belly through the undergrowth. He held his hands over his face and his ears, desperate to block it all out and to get as far away from the camp as possible, but he knew he couldn't. They had trusted him. Ethan visualized Giovanni telling him to relax. Ethan opened his eyes and they were red. He felt the transformation start to take place and ripped at his own skin as if something inside were trying to escape. He felt the power within himself and then the visions came and everything went silent.

Ethan was no longer in the middle of a war zone; instead, as he looked around, he realized he was back in a cave at the south of his location on the outskirts of a town called Oudshoorn. It was in the Western Cape province of South Africa. In those days, there had been a population of approximately 80,000 people. It was the largest town in the little Karoo region. Today, the population had been reduced to nothing. Nuclear fallout had taken its toll. His own parents had been killed.

Memories flooded his mind, drowning him in sudden sorrow. His thoughts became blurred, jumbled, but gradually cleared as he searched for the true vision. Ethan could see his parents fighting a man. Ethan could sense that in this vision, he was very young, so he was looking through the eyes of a child, but the memory now surged forward. The man wielded a sword and a dagger that looked like bronzed wood. Ethan's parents fought but the other man was too strong, his movements were hypnotic and compelling. His eyes were filled with a blood lust. He had destroyed Ethan's parents and had disappeared in the night just as fast as he had appeared.

Ethan had an idea that Paxton was the hunter who had killed his parents but he did not want to believe it. He felt sick for even considering it. There was just a familiarity that he could not ignore. Ethan had not seen the face clearly, just the eyes, but he could feel somehow that Paxton had something to do with his parents' death. The visions always made him feel groggy and they were happening now at the worst possible time. He tried to push the memory out of his mind and to bring the image of the hunter back so he could see him more clearly. The memory faded. Ethan did not know if it was a dream or not, or if his memories of the past were true and returning to him. All he knew was that Gloria had trusted him to keep Paxton and Lars safe and he was going to do just that, there would be time later to solve the mystery of his parents' untimely death – if they managed to survive.

* * *

"Do you have any more silver bullets left?" I reached out to Lars discreetly as he quickly holstered one of his guns and reached for a clip from a sleeve in his pants pocket. He threw it to me as the werewolves started to push forwards, driving us back towards the shack.

I had to jump for the clip, inserting it into the Glock, pulling back on the mechanism to load a round in the chamber, just as a werewolf grabbed my hand and knocked me off balance. He bit down, slicing his sharp teeth through the weapon and my finger. Pain tore through me. I knew the gun had taken the brunt of the

PROPHECY

force but the bone was going to break, I could feel the pressure and cried out in pain. I twisted awkwardly, trying to reach the kill instrument, which had been jolted from my hand during the collision. Werewolves didn't like to let go of their prey, they chomped down harder, locking their slavering jaws into position, and they held on. I searched desperately for the kill instrument, doubting my own ability to defend myself against this large werewolf. I was stuck against a large tree root that was preventing me from turning and getting hold of my weapon. The weight of the wolf bearing down on me was colossal.

I could feel the werewolf dragging me now and if I waited any longer, I was going to die. I flung out one arm towards the kill instrument and this time recited the words out loud. "HANDIS REGAMORTIS!" The words shot out like lighting as the kill instrument slid towards me on the ground, cutting through any obstacle in its way. Once it was in my hand, I dug down into the soil, slowing down the werewolf and giving me enough time and space to spring myself up into the air. That I had the kill instrument had not gone unnoticed. Two other werewolves were running in fluid motion towards me. I couldn't delay. I threw myself down onto the mouth of the first werewolf and with my free hand, took the handle of the kill instrument, pushing it up through the skin and sinewy muscles of the werewolf's neck, pushing the magazine into place. The werewolf gagged and yelped, releasing me so I could push the gun against its teeth, releasing the pin and chambering one of the rounds.

The werewolf was staring right at me. I knew that its vision was red-tainted, like looking through a colored lens. I couldn't help but wonder if this made me all the more appetizing. I fired two rounds straight into its brain. It released me immediately and I scrambled back. Out of the corner of my eye, I saw another wolf jumping for me and, springing to my feet like a cat, bounced from my position and spiraled around. I thrust the kill instrument under the werewolf's jaw, holding up its head, and fired a bullet went into the brain. Dead.

As I tried to recover my footing, I spotted yet another coming at me. This one had gained a vantage point and was dropping down onto me as I struggled to release the kill instrument that was still lodged in the other wolf's jaw. I prepared for impact and knew that Lars was aware of my situation but was trapped with 10 or more werewolves surrounding him.

I lost my sense of fear and in that moment came acceptance. I was ready to grapple with the werewolf. My chances of survival were slim as the werewolf had the high ground and the advantage of full strength and weight. I held up my arms as the wolf plunged towards me, my badly damaged hand with exposed innards acting like a beacon to the hungry werewolf.

I was seconds away from catching the werewolf in my bare arms but out of nowhere, a figure barreled into the werewolf, sending it careering off balance into the undergrowth. The impact had knocked me off balance too but somehow I manage to twist, staggering on uneven soil and saving myself – just. The werewolf was down but not out. It breathed heavily; I could hear it. Its rasping breath told me that it was badly injured. Droplets of drool sprayed as it staggered to its feet, shaking its head. I could see that every breath was painful and I guessed one lung had been punctured.

I spotted rustling in the bushes behind the werewolf; it seemed as if the figure had not disappeared but was coming back for more. It was over in seconds. The figure came at the werewolf so hard and so violently that it did not have a second to react. The creature tore at it like a rabid animal. It was pure rage and I could do nothing but watch. The vampire left nothing of the chest cavity. Its claws ripped out everything from the chest. The remnants were just a shell of the former animal.

Recognition suddenly dawned. I knew exactly who it was but before I could utter a word, my attention was diverted by the sound of other werewolves stalking us. They watched closely, looking for any signs of weakness, and I was vulnerable alone surrounded by this many deadly assassins. I glanced over at Lars noting he had bested at least six of the fully transformed werewolves since they were only half-breeds, but found it much more of a challenge when up against the two remaining purebloods with swords.

I watched as Lars took a chance to get across to me. We were stronger as a team and their defenses were limited. The opponents were superior in theory but we had both had come out of worse situations before.

I watched carefully, checking out my opponents. I had one eye on the approaching werewolves, but my main focus was on Lars. If he went down, my odds of survival were dramatically reduced. The attack on Lars was fast and frenzied. As they came in, one went high and one went low. As they slashed, Lars blocked the low blow, saving his kneecaps by an inch. Within the same motion, he ducked and spun around the other. In a blink of an eye, one werewolf decapitated its partner as Lars impaled the spin, crushing the heart from behind.

I moved towards the mystery werewolf killer. Somehow Ethan had connected with his inner beast but I had never seen a vampire change its form so distinctly. He was thicker and taller, a giant of a man with fangs. Ethan breathed in hard, seemingly still dazed. I reached out to touch him and ducked as he swiped at me. Recognition filtered through his rage and his facial expression changed from a deranged werewolf killer to a coherent boy. Ethan spoke, but this time his voice was lower, matured. The boy had come of age.

"Paxton, I am so sorry. I don't know what got into me. Can you ever forgive me?"

I placed a gentle hand on Ethan's shoulder, "Now is not the time to talk, Ethan, we are surrounded by werewolves and we need to retreat. There's a big fight ahead."

"I'll do what I can." Ethan vowed.

Lars had managed to join us, blood dripping down his face. "I guess there is no other option?"

I shook my head. "We have to fall back and that means we walk into the trap they have set for us."

We headed back towards the shack, twigs crackling underfoot. The werewolves closed in on us, blocking off any chance of escape through their numbers.

"Are you really sure about this? If we couldn't defeat this lot how can we defeat all that are waiting down there?" Lars queried, glancing around nervously.

"This might be a one-way trip but at least we will go down fighting." I looked at my companions, bloody, battered but still resilient. I knew they would be with me till the end.

We ventured in slowly, and very reluctantly. I turned to look back at the werewolves behind us. They had stopped and had formed a defensive barricade cutting off any chance of our retreating. We really did have no chance of escaping. There were enough of them to cover about 50 feet in either direction. I whispered to Lars, "Whoever set us up knew exactly where we would be, how many of us there were, and also how to match our fighting strength."

Lars looked over at Ethan, raising one eyebrow in a quizzical manner. Ethan had reverted back to his normal self although his outfit now resembled little in the way of clothes; it had ripped apart at the seams during his transformation to reveal his toned body. His rippling muscles held his loose pants up and made his chest look so much larger. He had changed in a multitude of ways and I realized that Ethan was coming into his own – just in time, I thought. For someone who had just ripped the chest cavity out of a werewolf, he seemed very self-conscious about his appearance. I wanted to mock him, but figured this wasn't the time and place.

I glanced out of the window noting that the wall of werewolves was still more than 30 feet away from the shack. We were well and truly trapped – as we were meant to be. I could hear the elevator whirring away and Ethan and Lars moved towards it. There were only two buttons: up and down. We hesitated; we had no idea what we would be facing if we went down there.

I suddenly became aware that my com-link was buzzing. As I went to take it out of my pocket, the wolves outside started snarling and howling, their attention distracted. Something had agitated them. The elevator doors suddenly snapped shut, with Lars jumping out just in time.

I flipped the com-link. Hayden. As I opened it up, I could see my good friend, his long, flowing red hair filling the screen. "I'd like to chat," I said dryly, "but we're in a pretty tight corner at the moment."

Hayden chuckled. "I know. I'm about to arrive to help you out."

"But how?"

"I have my ways to get past the law. You should hear me any second."

The sound of a helicopter approaching gave us enough time to run back outside while the werewolves were distracted. We still needed to kill some of the werewolves to enable him to get to us but before I could get into position, Hayden and the helicopter pilot were firing what appeared to be 30mm bullets that were filled with an acidic compound and liquid silver. This mixture, if shot center mass, didn't just enter the body of a werewolf; it infiltrated it and in the case of half-breeds, annihilated the body, releasing the silver and acidic compound before exiting. With approximately

PROPHECY

300 rounds fired per minute, there was a fairly good chance that Hayden could clear a path for us to escape.

We ran towards the helicopter as Hayden kept firing. The chopper hovered just a little off the ground, easy enough for Lars and Ethan to make the jump, but I would need a little more time. I pulled out my handguns and with the pin pulled back and a round in the chamber, started to fire at any werewolf that seemed to dodge the barrage of bullet spray. As Hayden came down to a safe height, a horde of fully transformed vampires came charging out of the shack. I pulled out a werewolf-made ultraviolet grenade – and repeated the mantra: pull, twist, and run like hell.

We had very few of these and they had never been used before. Gloria had advised me that we only had three grenades and they should be used sparingly and only in an emergency. I figured that eight fully transformed vampires coming at me with still at least a dozen very much alive werewolves vying for my head on a platter would be classed as a "dire emergency." Hayden dropped down to about 20 feet, and this was ample height for me to grab the bottom of the chopper.

As we took off, a werewolf clipped my leg; I felt the pain as a tooth embedded in my flesh, and I shook my leg hard to dislodge the grip that the werewolf had on me. I watched it fall with intense pleasure but this turned quickly to anger. It welled up until it crushed all sense of humanity. Someone would pay for this act of treason. It was someone within the council, it had to be, and we had essentially been sent to our deaths. I glanced out of the window as we rose sharply up and saw the grenade go off. The explosion was unbelievable, I saw bodies torn apart and blown many yards away. There was little left of the shack.

We had made it out of the hellhole at least. Thanks to Hayden. But the fact that we had a mole inside Safe Haven was worrying. The lives of everyone close to me depended on our solving this mystery and fast.

Chapter 5
The Enemy From Within

*****

"Keep your friends close and your enemies closer." - Tsun Tzu's "Art of War"

Lars couldn't think who had anything to gain within the Covenant of Light. The Children of Judas were a small group in comparison to the treaty between the Light and Dark covenants and yet, someone had dared to set up a trap of almighty proportions. PHLC owned everything and the Dark controlled it, with Catherine being the in-between person so the Dark didn't go rogue or become its own separate entity again.

Lars looked at Ethan. "It might be best to keep a low profile for a few days. Paxton is on a mission to rip someone to shreds for this."

"It can't be anyone from within," Ethan disputed. "Who would dare?"

Once off the plane, Lars stopped to brief one of the senior council members about the situation in Africa. It was customary to do so but Hayden, on the other hand, did not like to be told what to do. He did not report to anyone, and was loyal only to a few, doing what was necessary to save them. Paxton had saved his butt a few times so Hayden was just returning the favor. Other than that, he was a lone wolf and when he found what he was looking for, he would disappear.

* * *

Ethan scurried away like a mouse. Lars would not have warned him unless he knew Paxton was going to wreak havoc around the place. Ethan preferred the quiet life and was never fond of loud noises or large groups of people. Plus, guilt weighed heavily. He had almost cost the others their lives. Ethan knew he had to talk to someone about his situation. His innermost fears, the visions, the uncontrolled rage, and then of course, his unexplained transformation. None of it made sense. Ethan was on his way to find Giovanni – there was no one he trusted more. As he made his way down the side gate to the compound, Gastin appeared around the corner and quickly ushered him away.

"Come and tell me about the trip," Gastin said. "I think we have much to discuss. Giovanni is waiting – come."

* * *

I made my way directly to the command room where Gloria and Catherine were pacing the room waiting to see me.

"I knew we couldn't trust the Dark to deliver on the treaty," Gloria announced.

Catherine glared at her. "What makes you think that the leak is in the council?"

"Maybe because you allow so many people in this room," Gloria hissed scathingly, "and you leave doors open. I am surprised that more secrets have not escaped these walls."

PROPHECY

"This is absurd, Gloria. I would never allow anything like this. Do you think I would risk Paxton?"

Gloria ground her teeth, "I will have you know, that unlike the Covenant of Dark, the Covenant of Light is loyal and trustworthy. They have been brought together for one reason and that is to bring peace and balance between good and evil. If your 'people' can't keep their mouths shut, you ungrateful aristocrats, maybe we should break this treaty." Gloria paced up and down, taking advantage of Catherine's silence. "They have not once said anything to Paxton these past six months about what he has done to help them. He has taken out several of the factions that threatened their perfect way of life. They owe him thanks if not more."

It might be wrong to eavesdrop but I had heard enough. The last thing that we needed was for Catherine and Gloria to fall out. "Not quite the welcome home I would have anticipated," I said with more than a hint of sarcasm as I joined them.

Catherine's face lit up and she ran to my side. It felt so good to hold her again. I wrapped my arms around her and just allowed myself a moment of pure happiness.

"I am glad you are back safely, Paxton. But we do have some issues to resolve." Gloria stated the obvious, her annoyance rising to the surface. She sat down at the table nearby.

I untangled myself from Catherine's embrace – reluctantly. We sat down next to each other facing Gloria.

"How much did you hear?" Catherine asked.

"Enough," I replied. "Catherine, I hate to say this but I think Gloria is right – to a point. I believe the leak must have come from the council."

Catherine sighed. "I know you have every reason to doubt the council but couldn't it just as easily have come from the Covenant of Light?"

"Impossible," Gloria stated firmly. "I understand that you don't want to believe that any of those members could do this. We do however have to find out for sure."

"No one wants the truth more than me," Catherine retorted. "I am just not sure why anyone on the Council would consort with this group of renegades. They are dirty, egotistical, greedy, and evil, but their loyalties are financial ones."

"You are right, Catherine; they had nothing to gain, but more money. If they got Paxton out of the way they would assume more power and possibly overthrow us. You know they don't like being in an agreement with us. We are babysitters to adults – some of whom have been around for almost a thousand years if not longer."

I could tell by the jut of Catherine's jaw that she did not agree but was trying hard to not lose her temper. "As a member of the Covenant of Dark and Light, I know for a fact that our word is our bond and our bond holds our fate. Only true death can break it."

"That's what you believe – but does everyone feel that way?" Gloria shook her head in frustration.

I'd had enough. "We can't keep bickering. We need to find this person and we need to deal with it. Do you both hear me? I don't want to see either of you arguing again."

I could feel my adrenaline kicking in. I was angry. Rage bubbled up inside of me. Not at Gloria or Catherine but by the fact that someone had betrayed us. I needed some time alone. My head was starting to pound and our lucky escape was only now starting to kick in. I wasn't afraid of dying but I had come close to it this time.

* * *

The robed figure remained in the shadows. Only the sound from the com-link broke the heavy silence. A light flickered green through to red as the connection was made.

"Is this line secure?"

"I encrypted it myself."

"You failed me," the hooded figure hissed. "I gave you one simple task and you failed. I hardly dared to hope that you would be able to kill the werewolf and vampire and also capture Paxton Holt."

"What do you mean you didn't give me much hope?"

"As I stated. You had the perfect opportunity to prove yourself to me and you failed."

"You set me up to fail. It was all part of the master plan. To create deception and mistrust among the leadership of the Covenant of Light and Dark. I risked getting caught and facing death not for glory, but because you wanted to play a game. Well, no more. If I had known what was going to transpire then I would have never agreed to your crusade."

The hooded figure smiled a slow, menacing smile. "So you no longer wish to be a member of the council of the Covenant of Dark? That's fine, I will withdraw you from the covenant."

"No, no, that is to say I…I am sorry; I did not mean to speak out of turn." The figure knelt down, bowing its head in apology. "What can I do now? Go to the other plan we had in place?"

The hooded figure contemplated. "No, I understand you do not want those close to you to get hurt. I can't guarantee anything, but if you follow through, your place on the council is already set."

"How? The last member of the council to die was over 800 years old and he was destroyed during War World III."

Eerie laughter filtered through the com-link. "Leave that to me. You will have your reward and we will have a voice. One member is not enough either…Catherine has to be stopped or destroyed. The full plan can't go into effect until she is out of the picture." The hooded figure paused, then added, "Don't worry; we have ways of making people disappear. Pretty soon the day of reckoning will come."

The light faded as the connection was severed. The robed figure looked out of the window to see Paxton and Catherine together, their commitment to each other was obvious – their bodies moved in sync. Anger rose inside, it threatened to well up and spill over, to become obvious. The figure fought the surging tide back down. This anger had existed for many years, but it was not until now that the figure was ready to settle the score.

Chapter 6
Natural Selection

*****

Catherine and Gloria called a meeting of the senior members of the Covenant of Light and connected via the video screen to the Council of the Dark. Gloria had everyone seated with a brief in front of each of them – she was taking no chances. On the screen the Supreme Chancellor was not in attendance. Gloria raised an eyebrow; I knew she had expected everyone to be present. This was pretty serious after all. The council had held meetings before without him so this was not unusual in itself. But Ethan was also missing.

"Where is he?" Gloria hissed.

I ushered Gloria outside. "He's still in his room," I told her. "He was pretty shaken up by all that happened. I think he needs some time."

Gloria put her hand on my arm, she looked troubled and I watched intently as she trailed her hand across my bulging forearm, biceps, and then shoulder.

I moved back, perturbed by Gloria's intimate touch. "What are you doing?" I said sharply.

"What happened to us, Paxton? We were perfect together."

I recalled the relationship of sorts that Gloria and I had experienced when I was first at Safe Haven and didn't believe I had a future with Catherine because of her father. It was never a relationship, it was just two people alone and satisfying a primal need. "Stop," I told her sharply. "What I have with Catherine is real. It goes beyond just physical."

Gloria looked at me, her eyes saddened but brittle. She knew I was telling the truth.

She leaned in and kissed me. I pulled back immediately. My heart was pounding as her lips were insistent. I pushed her back, she was strong, and I struggled for a second to lock out my arms, keeping her back at a distance.

Catherine was in view. I could tell she was watching us. I also knew her eyes were widening and she was experiencing a multitude of emotions including shock.

"The meeting is about to begin." Catherine's voice was icy. "We could not find the Supreme Chancellor but his assistant will proceed and relay all in due course."

I disentangled myself from Gloria's arms. I couldn't read her expression but I had the feeling she had known Catherine was standing behind her. I had bigger problems: the Supreme Chancellor was the only one with the ability to bring about a new policy or law within the council. He was not the Supreme Chancellor by chance. He had been chosen many years earlier when the previous chancellor died. He was the next in line for the throne and currently the most powerful member on the council. He was even more powerful than Catherine.

PROPHECY

We walked into the room. I felt guilty, guilty as hell even though I was totally innocent. I noted Gloria walked past Catherine looking smug. I couldn't fathom what the hell was going on. I looked at Catherine through shocked eyes and then sat down by her side.

"I will discuss this with you later," she said, her eyes cold, "but first, we have a mole to try to uncover."

I felt like a naughty schoolboy, caught between my girlfriend and a former lover – but nothing could be further from the truth. I felt uncomfortable and wished I could be anywhere but here. "I am too old for this," I contemplated gloomily.

Catherine regained her composure, only I could sense the anger bubbling away inside of her. On the screen, the council was still missing Supreme Chancellor Joakim Fredrik. Assistant Chancellor Baldassare Vega spoke up. "In the Chancellor's absence, I will speak in his place."

Catherine's voice rang out clearly. "I am not going to sugarcoat the situation. We have a mole among us. This last trip was a complete set-up and we almost lost several of our valuable members. The attack was serious and precise."

"Are you accusing us, Catherine?" Vega said.

"No." Her voice was firm. "I sit on the council, remember? But information was leaked irrespective of this. We have to determine why and how."

"It seems you are accusing all of us of sharing secrets with a band of thugs that call themselves the Children of Judas." Vega's tone was clipped. "The fact remains that I think the council should take over this investigation. Either your group is not competent enough to handle it or you are so relaxed at your sanctuary of peace that someone took the information and cascaded it to our mutual enemy. Please, understand I am not ruling anyone out. We are taking measures to address this in-house."

Catherine looked at me and I shrugged, so she took over the conversation again. "Starting this week, each senior member of the Covenant of Light will be interviewed."

Lars quietly looked over at me and nodded acquiescence.

Catherine followed up her point. "Thereafter, you will all be interviewed by a very powerful telepath. A telepath will only search your mind for answers to her questions and she will ask you nothing else. If you answer truthfully she will know. If you close yourself out or are lying, you will be announced as guilty and we will proceed with additional hearings to determine your involvement."

The council members looked around and leaned in. Whispers could be heard from the speakers that connected to the giant screen.

"We are not sure if we can let this telepath perform such a search. I understand your need to search out the person responsible for leaking this information, but if your telepath tries to connect deeper without our knowing, then very important and current highly confidential information could come to light." Vega leaned forward in his chair. His face was stern. "We will perform our own inquiry."

PROPHECY

"This is not good enough," Catherine stated. "I would like this put to a vote. This is to preserve our way of life. This does not just affect the group who sit here but all of us."

The Assistant Chancellor looked at Catherine, saying, "I will talk this over with the Covenant and we will get back to you on this matter. Once Supreme Chancellor Joakim is back, we will set up a meeting with you."

Catherine nodded. "Thank you, Assistant Chancellor Baldassare. We appreciate your joining us and we look forward to our continued alliance."

The screen went dark and the speakers crackled briefly. Then all was quiet.

"Does anyone have any comments?" Catherine looked around the table. No one said a word against the idea but their faces mirrored their inner mistrust.

"Will Nina's daughter be the telepath who is hired for this?" I thought that she would have a little more sensitivity to the delicate situation. Nina had been a witch and a telepath who helped me in the past.

Catherine glanced at me. "I don't know yet, Paxton. It is possible – that's if they allow it."

* * *

A mere 10 miles from where the Covenant of Dark had just broadcast their meeting, the Supreme Chancellor relaxed in his armchair in his villa by the water. It was beautiful. A renovated manor, designed with a very artistic view of the world. The villa basically mirrored the effect of three rolling dice, each section slightly off center from the other in opposing directions. At first glance, the house seemed dangerous, unbalanced. But it had lasted over 130 years through tornadoes, hurricanes, and several earthquakes, and had only ever suffered minor damage. It was almost an abstract fortress of solitude for the Supreme Chancellor, but this night was different.

The Chancellor smiled in satisfaction as he poured a dark red liquid into his glass. It resembled red wine but was really the blood of a Swedish teenager. She had been the daughter of the woman the Supreme Chancellor was sleeping with. In his community, the lustful act would be seen as an atrocity and a scandal among the Covenant of Dark. It was not that being with a human was outlawed, but in a vampire society it was seen as unacceptable and would affect his status. The main reason he kept it hidden was that it might lead the council to either remove him or to give more power to Catherine. He would never accept such a change so it was kept as a dark and dirty secret. The Supreme Chancellor was drawn to humans. He had never felt the same passion with a vampire of his own stature as he did with a warm and willing human body by his side. This secret was never easy to keep so that was also the reason he had increased the security around him.

He spent most of his time in the study. It only had one window. He had arranged that the window had a steel screen to shield the room from light entering in during the day. Outside stood four pureblood werewolves on guard duty; they were sufficient enough to stop any intruder from entering the grounds. The grounds also had an alarm system. It could only be detected by vampires but it was enough to alert the Supreme Chancellor if someone was able to get past those

PROPHECY

defenses. Along with the alarm, the Supreme Chancellor had a safe room that was reinforced with a titanium and silver alloy to protect against werewolves. He had even considered the outer area of the room – he had installed a cleverly created defense mechanism that would spray a toxin, which was totally debilitating to vampires or werewolves. This would leave the intruder incapacitated until the silent alarm alerted more guards and several members of the council to aid in his safe return.

The Supreme Chancellor did not worry. With all of this, he was more protected than the presidents of some countries. He also had an age-old power. At over 1,000 years old, he was the oldest living vampire and with age had come supremacy, sneakiness, and an ever-growing need for power.

The Supreme Chancellor had several hours to relax before he had to make the journey to the Covenant of Light and their secluded meeting place. While he waited, he enjoyed the life of a dignitary. He listened to music and he drank a bottle of blood. He was living the life that many only dreamed of and relished it. His com-link sounded – a reminder from the council for the 12 o'clock call. He ignored it.

He sat back in his chair and continued to let the music take him to another time and place. A place and time when classical music did not come from a digital machine but from a piano and when music was live – it truly captured the soul, or would, if he'd had one. He even remembered Franz Liszt, Frederic Chopin, and Ludwig van Beethoven. He had met them all during their times. Nothing would ever replace being there live and hearing the music flow and then the roar of the crowd.

He drifted back in and out of the music – the face of Catherine filtering into his consciousness. He remembered how he'd had to listen to Catherine, daughter of Vigo. Vigo, son of Judas himself – he felt her level of entitlement was unwarranted other than her strong bloodline. Vigo was no more, so what right did she have? He poured himself some more blood and pushed it out of his mind as much as possible.

Stories of centuries gone by flowed through his mind. There was so much he had been unaware of – like Judas and his band of followers. He'd never had an inkling that Judas was more than simply a story. He knew of one thing that would be able to shed light on the history through time – the Hunters' Journal. But he himself couldn't translate it, nor would he ask for translations. It was the only true documentation that went back to the very beginning. He knew the stories and he knew the legend around it, but he had never seen anything to prove it.

He felt tipsy, off-balance. The pureness of the blood had intoxicated him and he needed to slow down. He was getting drunk.

"Supreme Chancellor, we have a slight problem, but…er…nothing for you to worry about." The voice was apologetic over the internal com-link. The Supreme Chancellor didn't even blink. Another false alarm no doubt, a stray pet from one of his neighbors or a bat flying into the fencing.

He chuckled to himself. If only the human neighbors realized just what lived among them. He would be an

PROPHECY

outcast or dead. In fact these divided nations might pull together and start a chain reaction that would see the destruction of the company and possibility the eradication of vampires and werewolves. The humans still outnumbered them a thousand to one. If each side came together as a united front, it might be the end of the species. But he knew that there would be many humans dead through him and licked his lips.

Turning his attention back to the problem at hand, he found out that true enough, the neighbor's dog had managed to get through the security fencing again. A guard found the dog, a regular size Labrador retriever. It was obviously dead – its chest cavity was carved open from stomach to neck. The smell of blood was pungent.

Lifting his com-link to call in, the guard only heard a slashing sound behind him before his head was cut clean off.

The com-link sounded. "Jack, come in, what's your 20, over?"

A lithe hooded figure dropped from the nearby tree, blood-drenched sword in hand. He moved deftly to the com-link. "Everything is fine, on my way back. I am getting some interference from over here."

"Well, I hope you got the dog. Hurry back to base."

The hooded figure in black was like a shadow as he wove in and out of the undergrowth. Around his neck he wore a braided chain made from hemlock. Hemlock was perfect for masking his scent. The hooded figure dispatched the guards one by one using a silver dagger and silver- tipped arrows as he made his way towards the house.

He entered the code to the door. Once inside, his mission was clear. He headed straight for the Supreme Chancellor. As he moved furtively down the hall, his intel stated that the Supreme Chancellor spent most of his time in his den. Like a shadow, he moved stealthily. He moved as if his feet never touched the ground. His plan was to take the Supreme Chancellor alive. The door was partially open and he could see the Supreme Chancellor partially slumped in an uncomfortable-looking position. Creeping up behind him was easy; the Supreme Chancellor was intoxicated by the blood wine. He silently withdrew his sword and then without warning plunged it directly into the chair from behind.

As he pushed the blade in deeper, he realized that there was no movement, no single sound of protest. He turned the chair around. A drained human, long dead, had been positioned for good effect.

A shadow moved behind him. "You have broken into the wrong house. I don't think you understand the magnitude of your situation."

"I was sent to bring you to my master. You either come with me alive or you come in a bag. The choice is yours." The hooded figure seemed unperturbed.

The Supreme Chancellor looked at him and flexed out his claws as he transformed. His body mass growing wider, he became an imposing threat. The hooded figure immediately took a defensive stance.

"Do you understand? I am one of the most powerful vampires alive. Do you think that you, a puny human

PROPHECY

man, can take me? I can smell your blood." The Supreme Chancellor listened for the sound of the heart rate to increase, but it was steady.

"Did you think you could scare me?" The hooded figure laughed. "You still do not know who or what I am. I am no mere mortal." His voice was disdainful. "I have been alive for almost two thousand years."

The Supreme Chancellor towered over the figure and showed no fear. "What are you, then? Share with me so that when you are dead I can know what I have killed."

The hooded figure laughed. "If you think you can kill me then you have not been paying attention. I am neither vampire nor werewolf. I do not grow old and if I am wounded, I heal. I am stronger than ten mortal men and can perform feats that can't be even comprehended by the most sophisticated of minds."

The Supreme Chancellor paused this time. His own internal system started to change; he felt a sudden rush of fear as he remembered an age-old prophecy, one which he had not believed to be true. When God created the hunter to keep the balance between good and evil, he also granted Lucifer the same respect, because if one side was too strong it could become corrupt. So a second hunter was prophesied to have been created. According to this prophecy the two would fight it out for supremacy for each side.

The Supreme Chancellor's red eyes bulged from his sockets. He looked right at the figure as the hood was pulled back and the face was revealed. It was the face of evil.

"It can't be, it's impossible," he uttered.

The hooded figure circled around the Supreme Chancellor. "Just call me the reaper and know that tonight I am here to collect – dead or alive."

The Supreme Chancellor wasted no time and attacked. His aggression and inner anger fueled each powerful blow that only just missed the hooded figure's head. He clawed at the shadowy features, feeling a spurt of blood emerge as his claws hit home. Within seconds, the wound began to pucker and heal.

"If you are some sort of hunter, you will die if I take your head." He lunged forward.

The hooded figure in black used his sword, parrying each blow with the razor-sharp tip. The Supreme Chancellor was able to get a clean swipe of him, sending his body hurtling through the air and crashing through a wall leading into the next room. He was slow to clamber to his feet, but did. The Supreme Chancellor had dealt with several hunters in his time, including dispensing with the hunter Igor Lovan in a battle that had taken several hours before the Supreme Chancellor was able to best him.

There were significant differences between these fighters. This hunter was half the size of Igor. He had been well over 6-foot-5, large but impressively quick. This man was smaller, maybe 5-foot-11 or 6-foot even. He might be smaller in size, but he had a supreme confidence and that did not arise out of nowhere. He would not take this hunter lightly.

He had not existed this long by just being powerful. He was highly intelligent and had an uncanny ability to sense his opponent's next move. The hooded figure had suffered a debilitating blow, there were broken bones in

PROPHECY

his right arm. Knowing he didn't have much time before the healing process started, however, the Supreme Chancellor attacked again. Taken aback by the ferocity of the attack, the hunter uttered several words with his other hand and waved his hand over the wound. A purple mist surrounded his sinewy arm and the Chancellor could practically hear the bones knitting back together. It was a spell to turn back time. Within seconds, the hooded figure in black got up and moved back into the shadows again. The Supreme Chancellor followed.

The Supreme Chancellor had been in similar situations in the past, and tried to anticipate his enemy's thoughts. He waited for his opportunity. His opponent, a mystery hunter, trained in self-defense and some sort of witchcraft, was a deadly opponent indeed.

The hooded figure in black gripped his sword and felt it in his hand. His anger increased, he fed off it. It nourished his body. It provided him with intense focus.

The Supreme Chancellor picked his moment and struck a powerful blow, ripping through drywall and bricks. His adversary was not there. He was using a spell that allowed him to stay invisible but the Supreme Chancellor could sense him. He was close. He sniffed at the air. The scent was stronger as he looked up. The hunter came down from the ceiling, materializing as he did so. He pushed his sword right through the chest of the Supreme Chancellor. It ripped through muscle, then bone and then through several organs, and he sunk to his knees gasping. The hooded figure landed softly but left the blade embedded in him, knowing it would limit the healing powers of the old vampire. While on the ground, pain tearing through every fiber of his being, the Supreme Chancellor looked up as the figure removed his hood completely.

He gasped. "It can't be you, we have an alliance. How could you do this? Where is your allegiance? When the council finds out there will be war once again between the Dark and the Light."

The figure said nothing, merely drew his sword.

"Please, take my money or I can give you power…name your price."

The sword came down on him, cutting through skin, tendons, ligaments, and bones with tremendous force until the Supreme Chancellor's body slid to the floor, blood pouring from the gaping wounds. The hunter reached down and grabbed the head, wrenching it free, placing it in a vinyl bag.

"You resisted, you fought me, and in the end I had to kill you. I do not know why at the final moment, you registered such shock. Soon I will end more like you. A storm is coming and nothing is going to stand in my way, nothing!"

Chapter 7
Ethan – 5 Years Earlier

*****

"You don't understand me," Annabelle said. "We are not leaving."

"No, I don't think you understand. Once the Covenant of Light has found him, they will take him away from you. You should let him come with us." The man sounded insistent.

She looked in fear at her maker – the one who had turned her. He gripped her shoulders by way of comfort. "Our son stays. If anyone tries to take him away, we will do what is needed to stop them." His eyes turned a blood-red and his voice deepened to emphasize his point.

"This is your last chance, join us in the Covenant of Dark and we will see to it that you are protected. Join our cause. Vigo does not like to ask twice. You know that you will be hearing from us again."

She stared at them, baring her teeth, and hissed like a cat.

As the men disappeared into the distance, Annabelle's eyes began to change back to cornflower blue, as did the man's. His eyes had a stronger and more dynamic color with a hint of green. They were different, fey –

alienated from the world, hiding in the canopy, unsafe, in a dangerous world. They were both worried, holding their son to them as they hid.

Their faces were all that were seen through a small opening. The moon was bright. In that one spot that shined through it was almost daylight. The woman reached out her hands to feel the light dance upon them; she knew that it was not warmth from the sun but the blue of the night –but it comforted her anyway. Annabelle recalled the days when she could feel the sun on her skin. Her husband, a vampire, had turned her. He had never known this feeling – he had been born a vampire. He didn't understand what was so beautiful about it. She loved how it used to wrap itself around her like a blanket and remembered feeling warm from the inside out.

Her son had received a rare gift, the rarest of all: He had the ability to walk during the daytime. It was during Ethan's youth some 40 years earlier that he left his underground home and ventured out into the daylight. Annabelle had shared a space with him. One day she awoke to find her young son gone. She had told him many times how the light was bad for him and that it would kill him if he were in it too long, but Ethan was curious, he did not listen. He had to see it for himself.

When Annabelle saw him walking outside she had frozen at first, fear rooting her to the spot, expecting to see him burn up under the beautiful golden rays. She wasn't sure when she had begun to fear the sun personally, during 200 years of hiding, but when she saw Ethan walk out into the light, she had rushed towards him.

PROPHECY

Immediately, her skin had started to burn, like molten wax. She grabbed him and ran inside. Her tear ducts blocked by the flames impaired her sight. Once inside, when her skin stopped burning and began to heal, she looked at little Ethan and realized that he did not have a single burn. She checked him all over, every part of skin, hair, and clothes, he was unscathed. Ethan moved back to the door and stood there with his eyes closed, embracing the sunlight, not burning under it. He was immune to it. This was truly a gift. Annabelle was scared but moved to wake her husband. He began to rush towards Ethan, but Annabelle stopped him.

"Watch," she said softly. "You see? He does not burn. The light does not faze him. It loves him, it comforts him...Is this why we were ordered to give him up to the Covenant?" Annabelle whispered and turned to her husband as fear welled up inside her. He was special and they weren't the only ones who knew it.

Vigo was willing to overlook their betrayal if they gave over their son freely. It was from this giving that he would gain the most power. Taking did not make his power grow; but offerings only increased the power of the Dark Covenant. Those that accepted his ways contributed to his growth. Annabelle and Edgar had no desire to return to that way of life. They wanted their son to grow up and be able to live a normal life, especially since he could emerge in daylight and experience a freedom that the others could only dream of. There were only two vampires who had the same gift and they were of royal blood.

Edgar and Annabelle knew that if he was captured, the Covenant would do one of two things with their son:

study him or kill him. The only other living Lightwalker was Catherine the daughter of Vigo and next in line to his empire. They would never experiment on Catherine, she was royal blood and Vigo, as evil and sinister as he was, saw his children as a reflection of himself.

* * *

The trees presented a perfect hideout not just for them but for their enemies too. Hidden in the canopies further down the isolated track, a man used high-powered night vision goggles to view the house and those that walked its perimeter. He had his orders. He was to eliminate the parents and capture the child. Swathed in dark clothes, and a hood adornment, he was packing guns, spikes, and swords. He was no ordinary man. He possessed many abilities including strength, speed, and immortality. He could only be terminated if someone were to get close enough to take his head, but in all the time he had been alive, only a few had come close enough to make the attempt. None had lived to tell the tale.

The hidden assassin stayed focused, noticing the son who appeared in the doorway. He looked like a 17-year-old boy but he was nearly 100 years old. The parents would soon be dead and he would have completed his mission. Putting on his head garb, he leaned forward, his eyes glowing ready for the blood lust. Power started surging through his body. He knew the parents would do all they could to protect their child. He was ready for that struggle.

***

Something was wrong. Edgar could feel it. The chill in the air carried danger with it. Their position was now too vulnerable. It was just a matter of time before they or the others would come. Edgar just hoped that Gastin, Giovanni, and Gloria had received his call for help. The Covenant of Light was his only hope of saving their son. Edgar looked around one more time, focusing his eyes on all the far reaches of the jungle outskirts...he had the strangest feeling that he was being watched.

Once inside, Edgar bolted the doors and the windows. The windows had a sliding metal shield that covered them from the light and also protected them from gunfire and other ammunition. The shack, although small, could take a pretty good attack and still withstand the brunt of it. Annabelle looked at Edgar as Ethan went back into his room to rest – he looked concerned. They both knew Ethan was special and that others wanted him, but didn't know if they wanted him dead or enslaved.

Edgar recalled when he and Annabelle were members of the Covenant of Dark. There was such a strong lust for power. It was never enough. The desire for more power sent them over the edge, causing anger, rage, destruction, and more. They had fought several battles against the Light, but they wanted out. It was not how they wanted to spend their eternity together. They wanted more out of it. They loved each other and it was that love that helped them realize there was a better way. Vigo ordered that they complete one more mission. Their last mission was to infiltrate the

Covenant of Light, to gain their trust and through this, discover several of their main installations.

As they started to gain the trust of the Light, they saw how wonderful it was. Love, respect, and the feeling of yet more power, but this was a true power. So Edgar and Annabelle came clean to Gloria and the Covenant of Light and made a deal with them. If the Light would accept them for who they had become and would let them live, they would share with them a very secretive installation that the Dark had put into production. This installation was set up to harvest humans in cryogenic chambers, which meant that they could be kept alive as either blood to feed on or as potential vampire soldiers for the coming war. Paxton had, along with the Covenant of Light, set up a mission to shut down this installation, and thanks to Annabelle and Edgar, they did just that. The one problem with this plan was that Vigo would know that Edgar and Annabelle had been involved in it. Their lives would always be in danger. Gloria had promised to set up a place to keep them safe.

Because of their original betrayal, the Covenant of Light declared that they could never know the location of Safe Haven, but promised to let them live. The Covenant of Light would always look out for them as long as they continued to prove they could follow the side of the Light. Edgar and Annabelle understood this and it was during this time that they were put into protective custody by the Light in Africa. Then Ethan was born. During this time in Africa, Edgar, Annabelle, and Ethan lived in peace. Ninety-four years had passed since they were sent to Africa. During this time only Gloria knew the wonderful things that were happening with them all. She was their link, the person who they

PROPHECY

turned to. It was around the 95th year that the Covenant of Dark found out that they were living in Africa. Vigo had hired witches as bounty hunters to find Edgar and Annabelle on the off-chance that they had survived the years and to ensure that they returned to pay for their crimes and to face true death.

It was during this time that these bounty hunters found an even greater prize, Ethan, as he had left his family home during the day. The light didn't even slightly burn him. It hugged his body like a shirt. This was a revelation and the information quickly was sent back to Vigo, who saw this as an opportunity to try to get the trust of Edgar and Annabelle so he could take this child of theirs. He needed them to willingly hand Ethan over so he could have full control of this child's abilities. Vigo's most loyal men were sent out to meet with them about their child. Gloria intercepted the call but was unsure whether the Council of Light would welcome Edgar and Annabelle into Safe Haven. Edgar didn't want refuge from Vigo. He just wanted Gloria to take their son and to protect him and his abilities. He was a worried father and knew that he couldn't keep Ethan with him. Gloria promised to do all she could do to help them and in the process try to keep Ethan's secret.

Gloria had to bring the mission before the Council of Light to approve the use of force to enter Africa. They all knew that it was a suicide mission, at least for the numbers that Gloria was looking for. She had anticipated at least 25 troops were needed for the mission. Twelve werewolves, 12 vampires and herself. She would have sent Paxton but this was her mission and besides, Paxton had been sent off on a classified mission elsewhere. The council had denied her mission to help her friends completely. She tried to gain support, but it was no use. Time was of the essence, however, and she needed to act fast. She would have to betray the Covenant of Light if she was going to save them. She called a meeting of those she trusted the most: Gastin, Giovanni, and Hayden, and begged them to go on the unapproved mission. After much deliberation they had agreed. Only Gastin still saw it as a terrible idea, but in all the time he had spent with Gloria, he knew her well enough to know that she herself wouldn't go if it was not of the utmost importance. So they prepared their rescue mission to Africa.

* * *

The dark figure prepared to attack the family down below. It was time. He was tired of waiting – screened in the canopies, it was an uncomfortable perch. Worse, he knew Edgar was suspicious and wary. They couldn't detect him from below but they sensed him somehow all the same. The hunter stretched and prepared his body for the challenge ahead. He had waited long enough to gain all the intel he needed. He was a purebred hunter. He knew the element of surprise was his greatest asset on this mission. Moving from his cramped position, he dropped lightly through the tree branches, maneuvering his body as he did so. He landed softly, the strong lower branches taking his weight. He sniffed the air. Something had changed.

There were few breaks in the canopy overhead but he could see the silver slivers of moonlight cascading through, penetrating the depths of foliage. His senses prickled. Danger was imminent. He'd always had a strange ability to sense danger – a sixth sense. He prepared his sword and made sure that the magazine in his gun was loaded. He pulled back the mechanism and chambered a round of wood bullets. There were five magazines on his leg holding 13 bullets each — some were wood-tipped and others were silver. He never prepared for just one type. There was always a chance for more.

All was quiet below, so he dropped down the last few yards, landing in stealth mode. He moved quietly, carefully, picking his way through the scrub towards the shack. The family was still up. Their hushed voices carried in the midnight air, Edgar and Annabelle were going to go out hunting for any intruder. Ethan was to take the tunnel to a cave – less than a mile away.

"Don't be scared, son," he heard Edgar say. "Control your fear. It is probably nothing. If not, your mother and I will deal with it. Whatever you do, don't come out, stay there and help will come. We love you."

The dark figure now clinging to the walls of the shack like a second skin smiled. It would be the last time they would ever speak with their son. As he prepared his body, he stiffened, there was danger but from outside of the shack. Vigo had sent his men to fetch Ethan. Frustration washed over him. He clung deeper into the shadows and blended while he observed. Four men approached, two began transforming into giant werewolves, and they were very close to him but totally unaware of his presence. He could see one of the wolves had one blue and one brown eye. This was unusual, to say the least. The other two men turned from their human form into vampires. As they walked, they split up, covering a larger expanse and blocking off any possible exit.

One of the vampires kicked hard at the front door. But it didn't budge. It was reinforced with steel. Edgar jumped off the roof, fully transformed. He caught the vampire in the neck, his teeth slicing through flesh, and punched his hand through his back, pulling his heart out, blood dripping over his hand. Edgar took it, biting down hard on it, squeezing out all of the blood and draining it. This was a power boost for vampires. Short-lived, but Edgar would utilize it to his advantage. One of the werewolves leapt at him as Edgar was devouring the heart, he yelped as sharp teeth sliced through skin and bone and knocked him off balance. The werewolf hurled him about 20 feet in the air, his body crashing against a tree.

Melting into the shadows, the dark figure just watched. It made sense for him to sit back and to let the numbers dwindle down before he came in for the kill. His mission was clear, collect the boy. The vampires and werewolves could destroy the parents and each other for all he cared. He would…

Annabelle jumped from the roof, slicing at his curved body where he had molded to the shack. He didn't know how she had detected him, but the evidence lay in the deep cuts across his back. He fell, rolling to his feet with both swords drawn.

"Did you really think we were unaware of your presence? We have lived in this place for almost a hundred years. We know if a leaf moves or drops to the floor."

PROPHECY

Annabelle came at him, claws drawn. He drew his sword, slashing at her, but she blocked his blow. She dove in with her mouth open and her teeth exposed, she was ready to bite down. He sidestepped her neatly, noticing that she had gone directly into the path of one of the large werewolves. The change in adversary did not faze her. Her lips bit through the fur of the werewolf and she locked on, clamping her jaw, starting to drain the werewolf. As Edgar had done only minutes before, she punched through its back, searching for its heart. Since it was a pureblood she couldn't remove its heart from its chest. So instead, her fury fueled by her need to protect her son, she tried to grab the shell around it and to crush it. Slowly, the bone started to crack. The werewolf fought back, but since its blood was being drained, it was growing ever weaker.

The figure in black quietly watching the battle drew his sword and pierced it directly through its chest. The blade shattered the bone that encased the heart. He spun around for momentum, lifting his blade, and then severed the head from the body. After impact, he didn't realize that his blade had shattered near the end. The way it had pierced the bone, it found a weak point within the metal.

Annabelle noticed that Edgar was pinned down. The larger vampire had buried his teeth deeply into Edgar's neck and was draining him. She screamed, watching Edgar's blood spurt in torrents as the vampire slurped and swallowed. She rushed over to him. Before she could reach Edgar, their eyes met. She noted his desperation and his acquiescence of death.

"Edgar. No!"

The vampire and werewolf, working together from each side, pulled at Edgar's weak body, the force ripping his body in half. With his heart exposed, the werewolf tore it out of his chest cavity and bit into it deeply, blood spurting out of its jaws. The figure in black lunged at the werewolf but mistimed and was thrown heavily to the ground. He was showered with Edgar's blood as the werewolf slobbered over him, his breath reeking of stale meat and decay. As it was opening its jaws, Annabelle was filled with rage. She sprang into action, forgetting to make sure Ethan was taking the passageway. She blindly rushed in, attacking the werewolf and knocking it away from the dark figure. With her power and sheer adrenaline, she caught the werewolf off-guard, reaching into its mouth as she held it off the ground by its throat. Squeezing hard, she witnessed its eyes bulging as she crushed the larynx and then ripped out its tongue. The werewolf died as she then proceeded to pull its head apart by separating the top and bottom jaw.

The figure in black called out to her as he rolled to one side avoiding the discarded werewolf as it slumped to the ground. His warning failed to save her. A vampire grabbed her from behind, trapping her in a headlock. He snapped her neck within seconds, watching her drop to the ground, slicing a blade through her neck, severing her head completely, her eyes shocked and staring as her head rolled across the floor.

All that remained was the dark figure and the vampire.

They circled each other. The dark figure sensed the strength of the vampire. But he had to be wary. The vampire began to revert to his normal form, but his teeth were still showing and his eyes glowed the deepest red. He rolled nimbly across the ground, picking up a sword as he did so. The dark figure responded, throwing down the broken sword, then pulling another deadly weapon from the pouch on his back. This sword was older and it meant more to him because he had taken it as a trophy in one of his greatest battles. He lived with honor. It may have been the only part of his humanity he had left. The pacing continued, both anticipating each other's weaknesses.

Finally, the vampire morphed back to full vampire form. He charged in, while the dark figure took a defensive pose and waited for an opening. Swords were raised and parried as the metal clunking sound reverberated up into the air, sending a flock of birds spiraling up from the canopy. Their strength was evenly matched along with their expertise; the vampire came back around again, this time going high and then low. Each blow was met with a defensive block. Each blow was tiring and sapping his energy. Suddenly he saw an opening and went for it.

The dark figure had planned it all along. He had been trained by one of the best. With his sword to his side, he waited. The vampire by his very nature sought out to destroy. He fed off the weak. He saw this as surrender, but it was more than that. As the vampire came running in, he started low to get the dark figure off balance, but this was the dark figure's plan. As the sword swung, the dark figure went into a spin in the air, bringing his sword up. He saw the blade of the vampire's sword just miss his face as he spun. On his way down, the vampire was swinging down from high above his head but his own blade was pointed straight up at the vampire's throat. The dark figure had planned well and sliced through the vampire's neck with ease, while the vampire's sword missed its mark and sliced only through the dark figure's left shoulder.

The vampire was stunned. He couldn't move. He experienced the emotion of fear; it flooded through him in torrents. The dark figure before him was encircling him. He kept both hands on the handle of the sword, needing both as his left shoulder had yet to heal, but knowing that his furtive moments were escalating the tension, he continued, smiling to himself as he moved nearer to his victim. He stopped before him finally, removing the hood that covered his face.

The vampire was startled. "You? Why?" He struggled to form the words. He knew the end was near and wanted it to be over. He couldn't move and knew he could never survive. "Finish me...please."

The dark figure obliged, slicing his sword through the head and then whisking the blade back out, slicing it back just under the jaw line. The head was severed completely from the body. A mere ten yards away, Ethan the young vampire had watched the demise of both his parents and the final thrust of the sword. But more, he had witnessed the dark figure's face. Fighting back his grief, he quickly closed the door, locking it securely, just as the hooded figure spun round and caught sight of the movement.

He pulled twin guns from their holders on his legs and ran firing at the door. With pinpoint accuracy his shots hit the lock, breaking the pins instantly. He crashed into the door with all his might, just in time to see Ethan enter into a tunnel. The dark figure reached in and grabbed him. He had a firm grip on Ethan's arm, and was in the process of pulling him towards him, his mission nearly completed, but then suddenly, it felt wrong. A strange feeling enveloped him, doubt, pity, sadness. He experienced a moment of hesitation and let Ethan struggle out of his hand. The sound of footsteps echoing throughout the tunnel came back to mock him. He could have followed but didn't. He should have hauled Ethan out of there but he hadn't. He was not sure why he weakened but the boy was merely running towards his own death, he could not survive.

* * *

Ethan finally came round, his vision slipping away from him. Back in the present, he realized that the solid foundations of his life to date had crumbled to dust and he had no idea of who he was anymore. His dreams had been confused, violent, and without meaning. He was overcome with grief and wanted to lash out at anyone who was near to him. He could remember being held down in a cage by a woman and several men, and then, just darkness. He felt exhausted; reliving the events had drained him of all his energy as he had experienced fear in its truest form. Floorboards were creaking outside the door, and Ethan leapt to his feet in defensive stance.

Paxton opened the door and walked in. Ethan immediately fell to the floor, his arms up defensively, his heart racing. Gloria and Gastin, who walked in just behind Paxton, raced over to Ethan. Gloria hugged him.

"It's okay. It's okay. You are safe." Gloria ushered Paxton back. "Please, just for now, stay back. I'm not sure what is wrong but something has triggered an emotional response."

"He looked like he had seen a ghost," Gastin remarked.

Gloria simply raised an eyebrow. "Indeed. We need to get to the bottom of it."

Chapter 8
Paradise Lost

*****

Gloria was conducting a meeting when Gastin stepped into the room. "Gloria, I need you to come with me. It is of an urgent nature and it really cannot wait."

He looked serious and she had never known him to interrupt her before. She nodded slowly and made her excuses. She followed Gastin quickly. "How did you learn of this?" she asked.

Gastin lowered his tone. "The council was unable to get hold of you or Catherine so reached out to me instead. This meeting is classified, Gloria, and only Catherine must be invited."

It was unheard of for Paxton not to be involved. Gloria had an ominous feeling.

Gloria knocked gently on the door. She knew that Catherine was attempting to catch up on some much needed sleep and didn't relish disturbing her. She let out a sigh of relief when she saw that Catherine was alone and awake. "Catherine, we have to go to a meeting right now. I don't know what it is about but your presence is requested. There's no time to delay."

***

There was no point keeping the meeting a secret. Too many people watched the three of them go into the conference room and noticed that the door was subsequently locked. Lars knew straight away something was up, even if only by Paxton's absence. He slipped away from his workstation quietly. It took him a while to locate his friend who had ventured outside the walls of Safe Haven.

Paxton seemed deep in thought, troubled. He was working on different techniques and how to improve the element of surprise. Learning how to improve meant watching nature and absorbing the techniques of both the hunted and the hunter. Lars was fascinated. Paxton was scrutinizing the movements of a rabbit. He set himself up to catch it. He was now the predator, stealthy movements required, staying downwind, he got closer and then was upon it. The rabbit's frightened eyes fixated on him. He first had imagined grabbing it and killing it, but he couldn't.

"Life is not easy, my friend," Paxton murmured. "We all have to make tough decisions. Sometimes the decisions we make may not be right at the time but they always work themselves out." Paxton put down the rabbit and watched it run as fast as its little powerful legs would take it.

Lars moved nearer. He wished he could help his friend. He watched him walk in the trail that the rabbit had left. Even Paxton's posture belied a secret, regret, or a troubled conscience. Walking quietly, Lars followed in his friend's footsteps.

* * *

It's hard to have a tortured soul and yet to not know why. I had been experiencing a deep sense of loss of late and yet to my knowledge had not lost anything. I didn't feel right though. It was as if a part of me was missing. I was also experiencing the most painful headaches of my life. At times the pain was overwhelming. It certainly wasn't making my relationship with Catherine any easier.

I felt lost. Like someone had taken something from me. Following the rabbit through this myriad of trails gave me back something deeply comforting, a connection to nature. Maybe that was why I couldn't hurt the rabbit. It didn't need to die and I certainly wasn't hungry. Looking across the trails I saw a form, a shadowy figure. I blinked and it dissipated and I wondered for a second if I was going mad. Maybe the shadows were playing tricks on me but for a second I could have sworn someone was there.

A faint outline of a figure appeared to the right of the trail; it shimmered, beckoning to me. I drew my sword and made my way towards it. The kill instrument wasn't silver or oak; it was just plain, just like any other piece of wood. As I followed this elusive shadow, I found that I was standing before a brook; the water tumbled over stones in places but was mesmerizing. I felt so drawn to it. As I bent down to stare into the waters, I felt the hypnotic rhythm and gazed upon my face. My light olive tone and greenish yellow eyes were mirrored there, but it was like looking at a shadow of my former self, a shell, it simply wasn't me anymore.

* * *

In the conference room, there was serious news.

"We had a death last night – I'm afraid it was the Supreme Chancellor Joakim," Josiah Black reported. "He was slaughtered in his home. Several important papers were taken along with his head."

Gloria gasped and turned to Gastin for comfort. She had never really known the Supreme Chancellor but he was someone that helped them to work out their problems. He had helped to formulate the treaty.

Catherine spoke up, "We are truly sorry for your loss and as part of the treaty would like to offer our support in finding the murderer."

The newly appointed Supreme Chancellor Baldassare Vega responded. "We found evidence on the contrary, Catherine. All the evidence points to a hunter. There is no mistake."

Catherine didn't even take a second to retaliate. "You cannot possibly think that Paxton is behind this. He is the only known hunter and he would never, ever do this."

"Are you sure? We have been keeping a close eye on him and he has been pretty erratic since the ambush. He made it clear that he would bring someone to justice."

Catherine collected her thoughts, she knew it couldn't be Paxton but why would they think that he would do anything like this? Were the councils beginning to fracture apart and was the treaty diminishing?

"You just need to know that we have absolute proof," the new Supreme Chancellor said. He nodded for a

PROPHECY

recording of the murder to be played. The video showed a hooded figure, and they watched with shock as the dance of death was played out before them. Just before taking the Supreme Chancellor's life, the hooded figure revealed his face. The camera did not have a direct view of it but from the side it definitely resembled Paxton.

Brandishing a sword, he put one leg on the chest of the Supreme Chancellor, pinning him down as he begged for mercy. He then struck the neck of the former Supreme Chancellor, taking his head clean off.

Catherine, Gloria, and Gastin stood silently, shocked to the core. They could not drag their gaze from the screen. His face would have been clearly visible in the opposite direction, but as he turned slowly, the hood was replaced and his features went dark. He could not be completely identified. Catherine spoke up. "Someone trying to break up the treaty could have doctored the tape. It is obviously someone else. We did not have a full look at the face."

Gastin looked down at the built-in analyzer, which analyzed the last frames. "Catherine, it's a 75% match."

The new Supreme Chancellor spoke again. "To show you that we had nothing to do with this, we are appointing one of your members to our council to be a clear-cut representative of the Covenant of Light. Gastin, you will be a sworn-in representative. Please inform us of your new status."

Gastin looked shocked but did as he was asked. "I am Gastin – chief diplomat to the Covenant of Light."

"This is an unprecedented day. Never has a pureblood werewolf sat on the council and please take this in good faith as our non-involvement in the attempted assassination of your men in Africa...Bring Paxton to us and we will guarantee that he receives a fair trial."

"No," Catherine stated firmly. "We will start our own investigation and deal with this in-house. If he is found guilty he will be sentenced to 200 years below ground. At which point we will then re-evaluate his standing."

"This is not good enough for us. We demand that you send him to us. I am putting this in your capable hands, Gastin, to make sure it is done."

"Yes, Supreme Chancellor." Gastin looked guiltily at Catherine.

"Oh and Catherine..." the Supreme Chancellor stated, "if you do not comply with this, we will see this as an act of war and the treaty will be dissolved. You have our word that we will come looking for him and for your Safe Haven." The screen went dark and crackled as it went off.

"Gastin, how could you agree to this?" Catherine was incredulous.

"I did not have a choice. You are lucky they are granting us another voice on this. I cannot do anything if my first order on the council is to disobey the council. Let me figure this out. There has to be a logical explanation for why Paxton showed up on those tapes."

Catherine looked at Gloria. "Where is Paxton?"

"I think he is outside the perimeter right now."

PROPHECY

"I will do all I can for Paxton. You both know that but we have to lock him up and allow the trial to take place while we investigate for ourselves."

Catherine pulled up the com-link as Gastin walked out of the door. He paused long enough to hear her order.

"All werewolves and Vampire Guards, you are to apprehend Paxton and bring him to Cell 1176. This is a code 7."

Gastin heard it and then hurried off. He wanted to get to Paxton before the others if he could.

Catherine closed the com-link as she fell to her knees in tears. She had just called for the capture of the man she loved above all else. She felt helpless and frustrated. What could she do to save him?

* * *

Gastin went to the armory where he knew Lars would be sharpening tools. "Do you know where Paxton is?"

Lars glanced up. "Yes, just outside the rear entrance. Gate 6. Why? Gastin, is something wrong? Your heart rate is elevated and you are sweating."

"You need to deliver him a message for me. We have reason to believe that Paxton in retaliation killed the Covenant of Dark's Supreme Chancellor. We have to take him into custody."

Lars paused as a look of shock and disbelief came over his face. "No, that cannot be true. Paxton has done some pretty bad things in his time, he has had to do some pretty bad things but he would never kill in cold blood."

Gastin sighed. He wasn't surprised that Lars felt a strong loyalty to Paxton. He pulled up the com-link, which showed the killing of the Supreme Chancellor. Lars shook his head. "It looks similar to Paxton, I grant you, but the angle wasn't good and it was dark. It could even have been a shape shifter or a witch."

"I want to believe that as well, but even the most powerful witch would need more than sorcery to take down a thousand-plus-year-old vampire, especially one as gifted as Joakim Fredrik. Lars, you can't tell the others any of this...I think I may be able to prove he is innocent but you have to play along."

Gastin brushed back his hair as he gazed out into the beyond. "Let me find out what I can first. But I need you to get this message to Paxton quickly before the guards find him. Hand him the keys to the bike and tell him to get out of Canada and to hide. Also, give him this com-link and tell him to get rid of his other com-link since they can trace it. I have this encrypted. I did it myself."

Lars nodded and set off quickly, keeping a watchful eye out for hunting werewolves. Gastin made his way quickly back up to put his plan into action.

* * *

The sight of my reflection was perturbing and mesmerizing at the same time. I was struggling to draw back. I felt a tug at on my thigh and watched the kill instrument turn to solid oak. Instinct took over and I pulled my sword, rolling to the side prepared.

"Lars! You idiot. I could have killed you." I knew straightaway that something was wrong.

"Paxton, there is no time to tell you all of the details but someone killed the Supreme Chancellor and they have your face – or at least someone who looks like you – on video committing the crime."

"What?" I cried. "I have no clue where any of them live or even where the council meetings are held. They don't tell Catherine until she exits the car that she came in and they move it each time."

"I believe you," Lars said. "They have ordered Catherine to turn you in to the Covenant of Dark to stand trial."

"That's suicide! They just want me out of the way! But why?"

"Gastin told me to warn you and he gave you these keys to the bike. There is enough gas in it to get you to the American border. The rest is up to you. I will help to create a distraction. We can work on your defense once you are out of the way! Take this com-link and get rid of yours. It's traceable."

"No!" I refused. "I appreciate you looking out for me but…"

"Paxton. There is no alternative. Give us some time to clear your name."

He was right but I didn't want to run. I took the com-link from Lars and slipped it into my pocket. He held out his hand for my old com-link and I handed it over, watching him stamp on it. It splintered into multiple pieces. They could no longer trace me.

"Give Catherine a message. Tell her to remember where we first kissed."

Lars looked at me, puzzled.

"Just tell her. It's best you don't know but she will understand." I walked to the bike and got myself ready for the take-off. It was difficult to leave but they were right, I had to go. I cast a final glance at Safe Haven, the one place where I had truly belonged, then revved up leaving only a trail of smoke in my wake.

Chapter 9
There Is No Place Like Home

*****

Catherine and Gloria received word that Paxton had fled the grounds of Safe Haven.

"I don't believe it!" Catherine was confused. "This will just make him look guilty!"

Gloria paced the room, saying, "I have given up trying to figure him out. Paxton has always lived by his own rules. We have to persuade him to give himself up."

"You sound as if you want him to be trapped in a cage surrounded by werewolves and vampires," Catherine accused.

"If he doesn't, the Covenant of Dark voids the treaty, declares war, and goes after Paxton with all of their force."

Catharine felt the weight of the world on her shoulders. One part of her was desperate to help Paxton and the other dedicated to her obligation to the Dark and Light Covenants.

"We were instructed to bring him in. I don't like it any more than you but we can fight for his innocence while the trial gets underway. Do you think I really want him locked up?" Gloria reasoned.

"I know you love him, Gloria. I am not stupid. I have been alive almost as long as you and I can see what it looks like when a woman deeply loves someone. I have that same look when I see him."

Gloria shrugged. "I admit sometimes I am tempted to test his feelings for you but I know really it is pointless. He has those eyes for you as well. Regardless of my feelings for him and my jealousy of you, we need to work together to find him. Someone knows something and maybe Paxton came into contact with whomever or whatever killed the Supreme Chancellor."

* * *

Gastin met up with Lars. "Did he get away?"

Lars nodded. "Reluctantly though. Do you think we should tell Catherine and Gloria what we did?"

Gastin shook his head. "We would simply get locked up ourselves and then how would we help him?"

"You have a plan, I take it?"

"Lars, you have to listen to me carefully since what you say may help us try to locate Paxton before anyone else can. Did he tell you where he was going?"

"No. He didn't. He just got on the bike and left."

Gastin knew that Lars did not lie convincingly so he really didn't know. He kept his voice low and moved conspiratorially closer to Lars. "We have maybe 24 hours before the Covenant of Dark finds out he is not in our custody and they send their dogs out to find him."

"He did say to remind Catherine where they first kissed. Do you know where that is?"

PROPHECY

Gastin had an idea, perhaps not the exact place but at least a state and town, Scott's City, Kansas, U.S.A. "It's where it all began," he whispered, more to himself than to Lars. "We keep the information that we find out to ourselves."

Gastin returned to the command room.

"We have werewolves out searching the area but no sign yet of Paxton or where he is heading," Catherine was saying. She had composed herself and Gloria was already looking at a map of the area and border of Canada and the U.S.

"As a representative on the council I have to tell them what has happened," he said.

Catherine looked at Gastin aghast. "As our friend for all of these years, I ask that you hold off for at least a day. Give us a chance to find him."

Gastin nodded. "As you wish. I will hold off for 24 hours. You have to remember that there is more at stake here than Paxton. This entire Covenant will be in danger of an all-out war. We all know how well that went before this treaty."

Gloria and Catherine were both worried. They cast shy glances at each other, not wishing to see the pain etched in each other's eyes. They both pushed their inner fears to the back of their minds. They had to focus on finding Paxton before Gastin went to the Covenant of Dark with the news that he was gone.

"I have to get out of here for a bit," Catherine said.

"I would like to walk with you. I will have to come up with an excuse in the meantime so as to stall the Covenant of Dark," Gastin requested.

They walked together down a large hallway that deviated into a fork leading up two separate stairwells. Before they parted, Catherine looked over at Gastin and said, "Paxton is lucky to have a friend like you. I know holding off telling the Covenant is a difficult one for you. They put you in an impossible situation."

Gastin smiled and said, "Well, let's just focus on finding him before we have to tell the Dark. I'm not looking forward to revealing that little nugget of truth."

She touched his arm lightly and smiled as she turned down her own corridor. Then the smile faded abruptly. The walk to her room seemed to take longer than usual. Suspicion and trepidation hung in the air. She missed Paxton already and had no idea when or if they would be reunited.

She entered her room, closing the door softly behind her, and her senses kicked in immediately. Something was wrong. There was a smell, a taste in the air that was different. Catherine turned to her full form. Her body elongated, her teeth sharpened, she was ready to rip into the neck of anyone who got in her way. Adrenaline coursing through her veins made her power unstoppable. She was no longer in the room to intimidate but to maim and then kill. A figure materialized from behind the ornate screen in her room. It was hard to recognize anyone when all she could see was blood-red and a pumping heart that sang out to her.

"Catherine. It's me, Lars. I'm not here to fight you. I have a message from Paxton."

Her inner demon was almost at its zenith but hearing Paxton's name, her human side started to gain recognition. Paxton. She focused on her feelings for her husband and gradually fought her dark instinctive anger under control. His name was like an antidote to the darkness within.

Paxton, she groaned in her mind. Paxton, where are you? Her anger ebbed away and she realized that she stood partially naked in front of Lars, her clothes ripped from the vampiric changes. Lars came over with a robe and covered her up. Lars held high respect for her and Paxton and took the approach a brother or a father would take looking at their child naked.

Catherine hugged Lars. "What is the message? Is he okay? Why did he run?"

"He ran because Gastin and I told him to."

Catherine was shocked. "Why would you do that, Lars?"

"To protect him. Gastin and I think that the tape was fixed. We did it to protect him so we could find out if it were true or not."

Catherine looked at Lars sternly. "So you aided him in his escape?"

Lars wondered if Catherine was going to turn him in. "Catherine, wait, I can explain why we…"

"No need to explain. I should be thanking you for putting yourself on the line. I'm just surprised about Gastin."

"Gastin said they would wait at least a day," Lars reminded her. "There is one problem. Gastin did not want you or anyone else to know what we were doing."

Catherine was a little taken aback by this but thought Gastin was just looking out for Paxton's best interests. "OK," she agreed. "I will not tell him that I know anything but I appreciate you telling me."

* * *

Safe in a room overlooking rugged cliffs and beautiful seascapes, a man opened his com-link, energy crackling as a connection was made.

"Is it done?" The voice was insistent, demanding.

"Yes," the man in the room confirmed.

"Does anyone suspect your involvement?"

"No, I have remained impartial and fair in my stance, no one suspects anything."

The voice crackled. "I don't need all the details. I just need to know if they trust you."

The video link between the two was not clear, but as the man moved forward, the image became clearer. His face was still hidden and his voice changed via a modulator. The modulator was encrypted so performing a voice match to anyone was impossible. His eyes were the deepest red, however; they glowed eerily. "Finish this and all that you have asked for will be yours."

The man in the room breathed a sigh of relief. "And the woman I love?"

"She will be yours," he assured him. "Deliver this message directly to my contact in the council, he will know what to do next. The actions of the few will trigger the actions of the many. This is exactly how I had envisioned it. Now I am sending you the final details that have to be delivered to my loyal servant."

The man in the room nodded to the image over the com-link and then inserted a small disk drive into it. As the file started to transfer, an indicator on the drive showed the percentage increase. Within seconds the indicator was at 99%. Just below the drive was a spot for a fingerprint scan which confirmed the identity of the individual receiving the files. He placed his index finger on the scanner and the color stayed a constant red until verification of identity was complete. Now the file was 100% transferred. The challenge now was to get the file to the member of the council. This would be no easy task.

* * *

Catherine knew where Paxton was going. How could she forget it? It was the first place they had really kissed. It had consolidated her feelings for him. In her mind she said it, "Scott's City, the park." She knew only a few people were aware of the location. Catherine wondered why he would head there. Then it came to her, if someone was trying to set him up, they would figure it out. If the mole was in the Covenant of Light they would know. If in 24 hours this information was shared with the Covenant of Dark and they turned up, then without a doubt someone was feeding them the information. Catherine paused. She realized she couldn't go nor could Lars. It would draw too much attention to them. She knew there was only one other person that Paxton still trusted and that was Hayden.

This made the most sense, Catherine realized. Hayden had come and gone at will for over 150 years if not longer. He lived for danger and was one of the most faithful of their friends.

Catherine considered telling Gloria but her feelings for her were still marred by the recent revelations. Hayden was the only other person she could tell at this time. Trying not to draw attention to herself, she indirectly sent for Lars and informed him of her plan. He agreed that it made the most sense. He left her quarters discreetly, ensuring that no one saw him. Retracing his steps and backtracking, he ensured he was not followed.

He finally met up with Hayden. "Your services are required"

Hayden was sitting drinking a bottle of one of the few remaining fine wines of the region that had not been poisoned by war. Hayden looked at Lars and with a serious face. "Let me guess, you know where Paxton is and you want me to get to him before the council finds out?"

Lars was stunned. "How did you know?"

"Lars, you have to know that I have ears everywhere. Just when you think I am not around and you are all alone, believe me, I am watching."

"I'll remember that. But, seriously, we need you, old friend. Paxton needs you. I would never ask you to do this. This was straight from Catherine."

Hayden looked at Lars and got right up in his face. "I do this for Paxton, not for you or for her. He has been there for me even when I wasn't there for him. When my shortcomings were all anyone could see. He always saw past that. As far as I am concerned, I owe this to him." Hayden took another swig of wine. "Just give me a place and I will do the rest. I can track almost anything and anyone."

Lars gave him the details including that Paxton might be using Scott's City as a trap. He swore Hayden to the oath of secrets – an old tradition that was passed down from vampire to vampire or werewolf to vampire through the ages. It stated that even if captured and tortured to death, the secret died with them. Since sharing it with outsiders and living was worse than dying, Hayden swore to it and told Lars, "I will see you soon."

* * *

Gastin noticed that Hayden did not show up for their evening meeting and approached Lars and Catherine. "Catherine, have you seen Hayden?"

"No, I haven't seen him at all today."

Lars spoke up. "I saw him earlier but he had his pack with him. I think he took off."

Catherine sighed. "You know Hayden; he always goes on these random missions of his own. I just wish we were all here together at the moment. When we stand alone we are weaker."

Gastin agreed. It was true that Hayden was a law unto himself.

"Do you need him? Hayden is a part of this community, but our agreement is that he can come and go as he likes. Safe Haven stands by its Freedom Act to all vampires and werewolves alike."

Gastin paused. "I was just wondering since he was not in the meeting, I was thinking about sending out a team with Hayden to look for Paxton, to try to get him to somewhere safe."

Catherine placed her hand on his arm in silent gratitude.

Gastin walked away, glancing over his shoulder. "Just let me know if he returns."

* * *

I managed to make it to the border separating Canada and the United States. From my vantage point I could see several armed guards with old military-issue AK-47s. Taking a shot from one of those would hurt but it wouldn't kill me. Ten yards from the border, I spotted three decomposed bodies laid out as a warning. All three of them had been gunned down. This canceled out my first plan, which was to get shot, look dead, and let them bring my body over the wall. Since it was nearly dark, I didn't have much light left if I was going to come up with a plan that left minimal casualties and allowed for me to get in undetected.

Of course, plan B could easily have been to create a distraction. Within my arsenal of guns, I had a Glock 17 with an extended magazine. In my survival gear, I had a device that was created in the late 21st century but had undergone several alterations over the last 100 years. It was a robotic repair kit. This kit could be placed on a spot that had suffered a bullet wound and would clamp down on the entry point. It would then with a mini laser cut open the skin like a scalpel; next it would go in with a clip and a mini camera to retrieve as many of the fragments that were still there. This device could be set to auto retrieve, manual retrieve and to do half of the

PROPHECY

process. Since the device was not that small, it contained several pieces. The main one was the clamp that would expand by a remote that had a 40-yard range. This remote also contained the camera. It was used during War World III to help soldiers who were too far out for medical assistance and who were under enemy fire.

I wondered if I could set up the Glock with an expanded magazine so that I could distract the guards on the tower so they would think someone was firing on them. It was a good idea with a lot of risk, for example, what would I do if the gun jammed after the first shot? They would be more likely to send people out to look for the attacker. It was possible that only a few of the seven guards would come over while the other five held their post. There were so many variables, but I could see that these soldiers had been on this wall for a long time, and many of them were very young. I just had to get over the wall, and I saw the perfect spot to place the gun and noted a weak point in the wall. It was a calculated risk.

Now the wall was not just some eight-foot-high fence. This wall was over 20 feet in height and surrounded by at least 10 feet of razor-sharp barbwire. A normal man would most likely fall in the barbed wire, severing arteries or experiencing severe blood loss. I knew that my chances were good. It was just up to the seven soldiers to take the bait. I positioned myself in the darkness deep within the shadows.

I waited. The time ticked by slowly. I needed to get across that wall as soon as possible. I needed to be in place just in case I was being followed. I could not get it out of my mind that someone at Safe Haven was an enemy. I felt sad but more, I felt sick to my stomach if this were the case. Living with betrayal was beyond contemplation. I could hear a couple of the soldiers talking about the previous night's card game. They seemed relaxed and not expecting any trouble. I knew that the time to scale the wall was now. I pulled out the controller for the clamp and flipped open the mini screen. It was dark but I could see the middle part of the wall and one of the floodlights. It was pointed near one of the entrances. With the controller in hand, I flipped up the switch and then placed one finger on a mini joystick. Just below it was an expansion trigger to cause the clamps to expand. These clamps were designed to crack open a chest if enough force was put on them.

I figured I would only need about 20 pounds of pressure at 5- to 10-second intervals. With the magazine holding around 30 rounds, this should give me enough time to get over the wall. I pulled the trigger and the first round went off. The noise was impressive and I watched as three of the men dropped down from the wall and took up a defensive formation. Their reactions were good but they had no idea what was going on. They peered over the wall, just enough to try to make out what it was. I couldn't move yet since the other four men still held their post. It was in a defensive formation but they were still in the direct line of sight.

I groaned as two more men came to assist. Now there were six in my way. I had no option but to trigger the clamp sending round after round off the giant wall. Within minutes I had unloaded 20 rounds or so. I was trying to keep count at the same time as I was preparing to make my move. The six men slid over and

PROPHECY

concentrated their fire at the one spot where the gun was. Since they assumed it was one shooter, they thought if all of them concentrated their fire at the one spot they would be able to finish him or her off. Nice plan if it was accurate.

I took my chance and firing some more, made my way to the wall. I snagged my hand on one of the blades but used my strength and a knife to help me scale the wall. While I was climbing over, one of my swords came out of the holster and fell; it clattered blade down and stuck into the ground.

"Dammit," I thought. I might as well have laid a trail for anyone following me. I had to keep going though. I was up the top now and made my way over while the soldiers were still firing into the wooded area. The gun was hit on one of the last shots and fell to the ground. This jarred the clamp, loose leaving the gun with still one round left in the chamber.

I used the shadows to hide while I evaded the troops and had just crossed over from Estevan, which, in the 21st century, was the eighth-largest city in Saskatchewan, Canada. Over the wall safely, I entered into what was once North Dakota. There were three states to get through to before reaching my destination. But first, time to get out of the military camp.

There were troops everywhere and somehow I had to blend in. I couldn't just walk up to someone with a bag of guns and a sword over my shoulder and ask for directions. I had to hide my things somewhere safe. A quick change of clothes inside one of the bunkers was first on my list and once there, I grabbed a spare uniform and changed into it. It wasn't the best fit, being a little snug around my arms, chest, and thighs, but I had no time to complain. I left the bunker and crept along via several memorials, stopping at one represented by a soldier which read: "To all of those that fought to keep America safe, please let this soldier symbolize the strength and resolve of the people of the United States of America." Dated November 8, 2067.

It was made of steel and rock material and had almost a tomb lid. Below there were additional words: "Let this capsule that holds a piece of the world prior to the war forever be enshrined within, protected and safe from the elements."

Perfect. I used all my strength to remove the large bolts, and was just about finished when several soldiers walked by. I took my bag and sword, moving them out of sight as one stood over the shrine.

"Soldier, you are up late, what are you doing over here and not at your post?"

I started to reach for my knife. I had no desire to kill but I might have to if there was a chance that the alarm could be raised. I lowered my head signing my apologies.

"It's all right, I will not report you. We already had one casualty."

"Yes, Sir," I said.

"A lone gunman thought he was brave to fire onto the wall." The officer sighed. "What's your name, soldier?"

"Clay, Sir, Joe Clay," I lied.

"Well, Joe – get to your barracks. We are up at 600 hours. Several of you are heading to our base in District 8."

"District 8, Sir?"

"Well, son, you should know that, it was taught at the academy. It was formerly known as New Mexico, Texas, and Oklahoma. So you may be one of those that will have to go, so we will see if you are on the list in the morning. They never tell us before time who is going. You just prepare each time these transfers come up."

"I will go soon, Sir," I confirmed. "I would like to spend just a little more time at the shrine. It's important to remember."

"It is indeed, soldier." The officer nodded approvingly and he walked on.

I put my blade back into my holster, concealed in my pants. I then removed the cover to the capsule. Inside were books by Mark Twain, seeds from some significant plant, sealed butterflies, a honeycomb from a honeybee, and many other items that must have been among the few things recovered from the remains of the war. I put all that I could inside apart from the kill instrument and one of the Glocks. I knew if I was going to get to Kansas I had to be on that transport in the morning one way or another.

Chapter 10
The Council Decision

*****

Silence filtered throughout the corridors of Safe Haven. Catherine felt cold. She had barely slept, the bed feeling too empty without Paxton. The word was out and no one knew quite what to do. With Paxton accused of killing the Covenant of Dark's Supreme Chancellor Joakim Fredrik, everyone was shocked and disbelieving. The halls were empty. There were only a few werewolves on hand at Safe Haven. The rest had filtered beyond the walls, trying to find some clue about Paxton. Ethan, Lars, and Catherine sat quietly waiting for Gloria and Gastin to show up. Gastin had called the meeting to provide an update on either the capture or the whereabouts of Paxton.

Ethan paced back and forth. "I can't believe it. Lars, Catherine, you have to do something about this. You know Paxton would never jeopardize the treaty or kill someone for no reason, good or bad."

Catherine hung her head. She so wanted to tell him that she believed too and that she had sent Hayden to find Paxton. She just couldn't tell Ethan that yet. He was young, volatile, and still very unpredictable. Lars had seen his rage first-hand and knew that if he didn't settle down he could lose control.

Catherine stood up straight and went over to Ethan to reassure him. They would all be present when the council was finally told of Paxton's disappearance. Catherine knew this would not go down well with the council. They would want to step in and take over the chase for themselves, and with no guarantee that Paxton would be captured alive. She had to stay strong. Hayden at least had a head start on finding Paxton and he would have an ally too. Catherine had provided Hayden with an untraceable communicator. It was very old technology so it was harder to pick up since it had been discontinued over 125 years ago.

Gastin and Gloria entered the grand conference room. It was named after Abraham the hunter who had joined Desman and Gloria to form the Covenant of Light. It was fitting that its unity had lasted almost 500 years and yet now, the Covenant of Light and Dark was on the edge of breaking after only months.

Time ticked by slowly as they waited. There was no conversation, just the sound of stray branches tapping at the window as the wind jostled through the leaves and the sound of the clock ticking ominously, reminding them of what lay ahead. The screen began to crackle and flash, out of focus initially, but then the council came into view. Catherine sighed and prepared herself for what was to come. "Good day to you all," she said. "Shall we begin with today's order of business?"

The Supreme Chancellor Baldassare Vega looked at her with pure distaste. "Stop, Catherine. We know that you let him go. One of your group has helped him to escape."

"Wait." Catherine tried to interject.

"At this point," he spoke loudly over her attempt to be heard, "we have some intel that he is heading into the U.S. and so everything from this point will run through us. I hope I have your acceptance on this. If and when we find the individual or individuals responsible for letting Paxton escape, they will be tried alongside him as an accessory under the rules of the treaty. We have our best werewolves and vampires on the job right now. Our first order is to capture Paxton and present the evidence to a jury. Only a majority vote is required to complete sentence."

Catherine looked up at the Supreme Chancellor, bile rising in her throat. "You can't take this route. You know if you try to capture him, he will fight. Let one of us go down to wherever you think he is headed and let us persuade him to give himself up so he can receive a proper trial."

The council members looked around the room, Catherine could hear muted whispers.

"Against my better judgment and as a sign of good faith, we have deliberated over it and we will let you, Catherine, and one other, accompany our men in their search. We will let you decide who it's going to be. You have one hour to let us know who the traveling companion is to be and we will send a plane to you."

Catherine breathed a sigh of relief. At least if she were there, they would not attack Paxton.

"Thank you," she said. "I feel that our continued efforts together will help to increase our unity."

Lars and Ethan both stepped forward and offered to help. Catherine looked at them helplessly, temporarily lost.

"There are only two people in this room right now or even on this planet that Paxton would listen to and that's Catherine and Lars." Gloria said. She looked at Ethan and smiled ruefully. "I know you want to be there for him but this is how it has to be."

Catherine fought back her anger. Paxton. The thought of him being hunted down like some criminal, it ripped her in two. She could feel anger surging through her, claws extending. She fought back the impulse to give in to her wild side. Catherine nodded her agreement. "I think it is for the best that Lars comes with me. We will wait before announcing. Tell them too soon and they will find a reason to oppose it."

Gastin walked over to all of them. "I think that is a wise decision. You and Lars are the only ones that can stop this before it gets…hostile."

Catherine focused on her love for Paxton, but the waves of sickness cascaded over her at the same time. "I am sorry. I must go. I don't feel so well. I think it's all of this tension and the need to try to do what's right even if it feels so very wrong." Catherine left abruptly, Lars trailing her to make sure she made it back to her room. There was no doubt that she was taking the sequence of events hard.

As they left, Gastin spoke to Gloria. "I have something the council has given me to get done. I am going to retire to my room and work on that if I am not needed further. Perhaps you will make the announcement to the council, Gloria? As previously ordered by the council, I will also be attending and joining them on the flight."

Gloria experienced a crashing sense of doubt. This didn't seem right. There was just too much going on at once. Gloria hated feeling that things were spiraling out of control; she was missing some vital element in all of this. She had to think, consider all of the facts and lay them out like clues.

* * *

Catherine felt weak. Her legs felt shaky. She had recently fed but felt like she had not eaten in weeks. "Lars, can you get me something to drink? I need something really badly."

"It's the shock." He hurried out, heading for the blood bank. Catherine sat in her room feeling as if something was ripping at her insides. She felt faint, sick, but hungry. She needed some cool air, the room felt baking hot, and it was stifling her. She staggered to the window, leaning out, breathing in deeply, and feeling a rising tide of vomit swirling inside of her. Blood poured from her eyes, nose, and mouth, flowing like a hose on full blast. She felt her claws extend again, as she gripped the windowsill, ripping it away from the bricks. She had a large laceration in her skin. It started to heal but very slowly. Catherine felt confused. Was it the loss of so much blood all at once that was making her feel dizzy? Relieved of so much blood, she felt a little better, she was still hungry but the pain in her abdomen was so great, she fought against the urge to claw it out.

"What the hell?" Lars stopped in his tracks, as Catherine covered in her own blood turned towards him. He watched in horror as she started to rip at her chest. Her skin was changing; it became denser by the second. Even with her immense power, she was only making small lacerations in her flesh as it healed almost instantaneously. Lars rushed forward, pulling her arms away from her body.

* * *

Ethan could smell blood as he walked down the corridor. It was so strong. He had fed on his own kind before, but this odor was different. Ethan moved cautiously towards the room and watched Lars struggle to hold Catherine.

"Dammit Ethan, help me!" Lars yelled at him, panic etched across his face. "I am not strong enough to control her or stop her."

Ethan shut the door, locking it behind him, changing as he did so into his hulking self. He had been working with Giovanni to focus his power. Each step, strong, brooding, he grabbed Catherine's arms, utilizing his power with Lars'. With their combined efforts, they had her pinned. Ethan in his current form leaned down and smelled the blood from all around Catherine.

"Catherine," he began.

With tremendous force, she freed one arm and sliced at Lars, cutting him beneath one eye. He moved back with the sudden momentum and ferocity but he still battled for her free arm. Ethan grabbed her arms, channeling his strength, his grip tightening. "Stop! Before you hurt the baby!"

Catherine's anger ebbed away and she fell back, looking confused and exhausted.

"Baby?"

Ethan in his full form was very intimidating but he gently reached for her stomach and started to transform back. His normal hand cupped her stomach, comforting and in wonder.

"Yes," he said with a smile. "Can't you hear it?"

It seemed that only Ethan could hear it moving around, nestled inside of her. Catherine closed her eyes, focusing on her stomach, and then she felt it, the fluttering inside, its first movements.

Catherine looked at Lars and Ethan. "A baby," she said. She breathed heavily, tears rolling down her cheeks. "We must not tell a soul about this," she pleaded with them, frightened. "Anyone would want to see this union as an abomination."

They nodded slowly. It was just one more secret to carry.

Catherine looked at Lars. "Have you heard anything back from Hayden?"

He shook his head. "But it shouldn't be too long before Hayden reaches Paxton, assuming he is still at the park."

"Yes, I would stake my life on it," she said.

"Maybe it is best that I don't ask," Ethan murmured and Catherine nodded her agreement. "For your sake, yes – I think so."

* * *

Just beyond the bedroom door, Gastin heard every word. He smiled. The baby would make Catherine weak, and that would make an important difference. But he now knew the location of Paxton. Gastin walked to his room. It took him seconds to connect via the com-link.

"The prophecy is true," he announced. "She is with child. Also, we know where Paxton is."

A cloaked figure at the other end smiled, fangs showing. "Activate the next stage in our plan. Everything is aligning just as I had planned. Soon I will have Catherine, Paxton, and their unborn child."

Chapter 11
The Long Road

*****

It was impossible to sleep. I counted stars, the great expanse of sky comforting me. I tried to visualize Catherine and I imagined myself killing this impostor and being a free man once more. As the sun rose, I entered the barracks just as the other soldiers got up for the day, preparing for the call. It had been a long time since I had talked to another human. There were times when I myself forgot that I was human and not some supernatural being. I looked to my right; the captain came into the barracks holding a virtual board. The virtual board was transparent, but the back of it was designed to appear out of focus. This was because human eyes were unable to see better than 20/20 to focus past the blur. This was part of the virtual board's design so that secrets could remain safe.

As the captain touched the screen, he was able to click on a soldier's name and to review his photo and a bio list. Today he seemed impatient, however. "Come on, men, get to your feet and get in line. Today, you are going to hell. District 8 was one of the most active war zones in the United States. It is now referred to as the United Districts of America or UDA, unfortunately they are far from united. Chaos, poverty, and crime run the districts with the stationed soldiers in some cases looking the other way as crimes happen. It's no longer what the founding fathers had in mind when they helped build this country. District 8 makes all the other districts look like a nice dream."

I couldn't help but notice the scared faces. Most of them were just kids. I focused on the virtual board, using my advanced vision to see past the blurring on the screen. The soldier standing right across from me was on the list. I needed to take his place. The soldier next to me was called Brent Gomez.

"Hey buddy, your name is on the list but I have an offer for you. If you forget your name for just one day, I will take your place and you can stay here where it's safe."

He looked a little dubious, but relieved too. Brent nodded.

As the names were called out, the chosen men grabbed their bags and headed for a vehicle that looked like a tank with the upper chassis of a truck. The name of the vehicle was a TX2. When Brent's name was called, he looked like he'd had a change of heart. As he went to step forward, sweat dripping down his neck, I grabbed the bag ahead of him. "Right here, Sir," I said. "I am on my way."

I made my way out to the vehicle, glancing back at the real Gomez who was looking scared but relieved. I sat down among the other men. They all looked terrified. One of the other officers scanned us all, "I hate to say this, but there is a good chance that a third of you will die within the first few weeks."

For a motivational talk, it sucked, I thought. My expression must have told the officer what I was thinking.

"You should make it at least a month. You have that badass look," he muttered approvingly.

I did my best to not make eye contact. I had no intention of entering District 8. My stop was Scott's City, Kansas. I could hide out there for a few days or longer to figure this out. I just hoped that most of the place was still the same, but in the two centuries since my last visit, there was no knowing what remained.

We were underway. The vehicle churned over rough terrain. I thought about the last time I was in Kansas. I thought about my years with Grandmother, I was glad that she was secure at Safe Haven. I hoped that she would know that I was innocent. She knew me better than anyone, and I was confident that she would be loyal until the end. She was a kind woman, but ferocious in her defense of me. I prayed the council would leave her alone.

I wondered if the world would ever get back on track but doubted it somehow. It was hard enough to create a system to filter out all the nuclear fallout even this far into the future. With the lack of high-powered systems to fully rebuild the civilization to what it once was, restoration was likely to be many years away. Many of the district inhabitants used existing structures to turn them into communal housing. So some districts had more space and less destruction than others, so many people moved. Overpopulation was still rife in some areas.

PROPHECY

When the bombs hit, they centered on strategic points like California, Washington, D.C., Florida, Virginia, South Carolina, Chicago, and Seattle. These areas had military installations, pharmaceutical laboratories, and the highest population of people according to the 2040 census. Other factors also played into the decision but this was a game-changer because the United States, along with other countries in NATO alliances, caused the largest use of nuclear weapons ever in the war that had started over oil. In 2045, the world had over 7 billion people and by the time the war ended, 3.5 billion remained. Many were badly injured or lost. The world had lost so much – plant and animal life and even the ability to export raw material that would have been used to rebuild civilization.

The vehicle came juddering to a halt. We had been traveling for some time and a toilet break was due. I watched the soldiers scrambling out of the vehicle. A voice rang out from outside the TX2, "Private Gomez, you have less than three minutes to relieve yourself or you will have to attempt to go out the back as we are moving. Let me tell you. You will not come out dry." The officer laughed as I got out of the TX2. He stood a solid 5-foot-10, but I dwarfed him by at least 4 inches and 40 pounds of muscle.

This part of the UDA seemed to be untouched except for the fences and military installations all over. Most of the structures were made of wood instead of metal. This had to be due to the impact of export laws, I imagined. I looked around, this was once one of the lowest populated areas in the 21st century but, in the 22nd century, it had to be one of the most populated. After the bombs, anyone who had survived congregated together. Half of the districts that now existed were inhabited. Each nation had the right to protect its borders and ports with full force and without warning.

I felt for these people. I really did. Life was hard and death was imminent. I watched as a truck from the PHLC pulled in, leaving medical supplies. I could easily see how all the wars had profited vampires and werewolves. They were now the richest species in the world, selling their miracle cure to all and turning over huge profits. During the last 150 years, a new government was being formed. The socialist government. With a slight infusion of capitalism – since not all could own a piece of the pie, the poor worked the businesses instead of owning them, and taxes were not cheap since there was almost a 25% tax for protection. This was military protection for all the states. Most states were self-governed and had their own armies, but this led to conflict between the reformations of the new republic.

I looked down, watching as a small girl came up to me, asking for water. I couldn't refuse and leaned down, giving her some water from my flask. She smiled, her teeth surprisingly white against the dirt on her face. Before she could clasp it fully, one of the officers knocked it from her hands. "Soldiers, back on the truck."

I clenched my fists and could hear my knuckles cracking. It almost sounded like bones breaking.

The officer scolded me. "They get rations and so do we. We get a little more because we are military, but sometimes when we get them, we have to go a lot longer than they afford us. You need to conserve your

PROPHECY

rations." He sighed, shaking his head. "I get your sympathy for this girl but this is survival."

My anger dissolved. The officer was sincere. He was just trying to look out for me. I asked him, "What's your name, Sir?"

He looked surprised. "Harrison, John J. Harrison."

"Well, John J. Harrison, I ask that you give all my rations to the girl and her family. I don't need to eat." I emptied out my pack and handed over all my food to the officer, clambering back onto the TX2. "Thank you, Sir," I said.

I watched as the girl with wide eyes accepted the food supplies from John J. Harrison. She was nervous with him first but then her face lit up. She waved to me just before one of the officers in the back closed the tarp that hid us from the world outside.

I have lived my life behind a tarp for so many years, I reflected. I have lived in different worlds. The supernatural and the human. I allowed myself to think about the Covenant of Dark. I would have never imagined that they would be the world power, not by their superior strength, or their near invincibility, but by the monopoly they had formed from the chaos and death of war. Politics won in the end.

As we set off again, I thought about how much the world had changed. I could remember traveling through Nebraska, taking in the land and the old-fashioned feel to it. I remembered their intense love for their college football team. But after 200 years, although some of the structures remained, they didn't emit the same feeling of pride or of quality days gone by. They were tainted.

Grocery stores were now clinics and hotels had become apartment complexes. Some still had the old signs up, perhaps to preserve some of the history.

My mind went back to the young girl. No one had realized that she was a werewolf. I could smell it and sense it. I think she could tell that I was someone other than a soldier. There was a pact, which was taught to all of them, to never let the real world know about werewolves, vampires, witches, or hunters but even so, she had been drawn out of hiding by her thirst and had somehow trusted me.

Perhaps she could tell that I was not there to harm her. It's hard to conceal their secret when among humans. Once they hit puberty, their aging starts to slow down. Their longevity depends on how often they change to a werewolf. I pushed all that out of my mind.

"Hey Gomez," one of the soldiers moved in closer. In a whisper, he said, "I know that isn't your name."

I went to grab the soldier but he parried my arm. "I don't care what your name is, I am Jack Jones. You can call me just Jack."

I tried to assess whether he was friend or foe. "What can I help you with, Jack?"

"I saw what you tried to do for that young girl. They frown on that stuff, since they don't want us to develop any personal ties to people or places. See, each district has a threat level. Some are lower than others and the way they keep some of the lower ones in control is by eradicating all physical attachments. Order keeps peace. That's why we are never allowed to mingle with those that live where we go. There are four compounds per

PROPHECY

district that surround the perimeter of each of those districts."

"Why are you sharing all this with me?"

He shrugged. "I…I feel a need to do so. There is something about you, a person still inside you. All of us have lost that feeling. It is because of that I find myself compelled to tell you what is out there. Death, decaying life, anger, and hate. Man, it is all there."

Jack moved back and leaned against the side of the vehicle. "I was once like you, full of ambition, but over time they slowly burn it out of you. I have done many things I am not proud of, and that's why I accepted this trip not as a selectee but as a volunteer. Maybe someday, if there is a God, he will forgive me for all that I have done."

He lowered his head. I waited to see if there was more but he never glanced my way. It was as if he had never said a word.

I closed my eyes, and thought about Catherine and my friends. This was a crazy, crazy mess, but one I had seen before. When had I ever felt safe? When had I not been hunted? I could feel my eyes getting heavy; sleep was finally catching up with me. I felt exhausted. My exile, the sleepless night and this long, stuffy journey – I'd had enough. As I started to slip into the deepest slumber, I realized subconsciously that it was the first time in years that I hadn't slept with one eye open. Since the road I traveled on was far from safe, nothing seemed to matter. The threat if any at the moment was human and not werewolf or vampire. It had been so long that such a threat had been any worry to me that I knew I was safe, safer than I had been for a long time.

Chapter 12
Next Stop Scott's City, Kansas

*****

Back at Safe Haven, Catherine was awaiting her orders from the council. She asked Gloria, "Why do you think they changed the pick-up point?"

"They don't trust us. They don't trust you either."

Catherine nodded. That was certainly the truth. Guilt weighed heavily on her. She wondered if she could have done more to forge stronger ties between the two organizations.

Gloria told Catherine, "We haven't been the best partners in this agreement."

Catherine seemed surprised. "I think we did a good job keeping to the treaty."

Gloria chuckled and said, "Really, you mean how you let Paxton get away?"

"I did nothing of the sort."

Gloria softened. "Don't worry, Catherine, I would have done the same thing. You know there is no way in hell he will get a fair trial if they get him."

Catherine stared out of the window. "I know."

"Wait a minute, this is what they wanted all along," Gloria said. "They are playing us. This is a great way to divide us all and it's working."

"What do you mean? Maybe there is a little more involved but..."

Gloria shook her head. "What about the Children of Judas?"

Catherine stopped her. "After the ambush, there has been nothing about them. All our intel has gone blank. It was like they just disappeared completely off the face of the earth. When Paxton and the others arrived at their hideout there were maybe 30 of them – tops. All our intel specified that there could be in the tens of thousands and growing, but still only circumstantial."

Gloria started to settle down. She didn't want to admit to it but Catherine was making sense.

"We have nothing to prove their group was a decoy and we certainly don't have a reason," Catherine finished.

Gloria leaned against the wall, she folded her arms. "Who would have something to gain if they pitted the Covenant of Light against the Covenant of Dark?"

Catherine contemplated. "With this treaty everyone wins. Why would anyone try to pit the Covenant of Light and Dark against each other? Who has the resources or the power to do that?"

Gastin walked into the room, looking from one to the other. "What are you guys talking about?"

Gloria spoke softly, "We are just contemplating if there is a bigger picture to all that is happening. Perhaps there is a mole trying to force the Covenant of Light and Dark against each other."

Gastin laughed. "It's impossible. First of all, these people would have more than one mole, it would have to be many people, plus who would be strong enough to front such an attack?" He contemplated for a moment. "The only vampire that could have done that was your father, Catherine, or you."

"That's exactly what I was thinking!" Gloria looked accusingly at Catherine. "Gastin has a point. You really are the only one that could have done this."

Catherine, outraged, started to feel her claws sharpen, her body changing, and then both Gloria and Gastin burst into laughter.

"Catherine, we are kidding." Gloria smiled. "You would never do this and secondly, you have been in the spotlight as our main spokesperson since the treaty. You haven't had a second to even be with Paxton."

Catherine began to feel sick. She wasn't sure what Gloria was implying; there was some emphasis on the point but her head had started aching again and she felt a little weak. Catherine reached for her com-link.

"Lars, could you meet me upstairs in the study?" Catherine left the room without a backward glance. She didn't really care much what Gloria and Gastin might think of her.

Catherine met Lars. As he approached her, she collapsed. "I need food."

"The baby is exhausting you," Lars whispered. "How can you go on the plane like this?"

"I have to," she argued, tears welling up in her eyes. "Paxton needs me. I think the baby is growing very quickly, my body is struggling to share the blood."

Lars picked her up and carried her to the sofa in the study. "Don't move," Lars said, "I will get you blood from the blood bank."

"Not a word to anyone, Lars. I don't want them to know. If they find out they will ground me. You and I may be the only ones that can get Paxton back safely." Lars acknowledged the point, moving into a run towards the freezer for blood. He was worried about her and the outcome if her pregnancy was revealed.

Lars came back with two pints of blood. Catherine moaned as hunger surged through her. She grabbed them both, tearing into the bags, with blood trickling down from both sides of her face. In seconds, the bags were drained. "Lars, I need more." She leaned back against the pillow, weakness still flooding her system but feeling a little more together now.

Lars ran back to the freezer and came back with an additional three bags. He watched as she drained them quickly. Catherine could feel her strength coming back finally. She breathed a sigh of relief.

"Thank you, Lars," Catherine said, clasping his hands with her own. "You have been a good friend to Paxton and me."

"You are both my family now," Lars said, slightly embarrassed.

Catherine's com-link lit up. "It's Gloria." Catherine sat up and clicked the button to receive the message.

PROPHECY

"We have the new location, Catherine, but the new Supreme Chancellor is also on board."

Catherine drew her breath. "I don't understand why he would go on this mission. His protection is of the utmost importance."

"I don't understand it either." Gloria sounded worried.

Catherine clicked the off button and said to Lars, "I guess it's time to go. Maybe I should stock up on some extra blood in case baby starts to act up again. I have a feeling I am going to need every ounce of my strength."

At the landing site, Catherine, Gloria, Lars, Ethan, and Gastin stood in silence, watching as the plane landed. It was very hard to see in the dark and the engine purred like a well-fed panther. The plane was all black and even the windows were a UV sensitive glass, which allowed for the appearance of the sun's rays to get through but they didn't actually penetrate. As dark as the windows were, it looked like just another military-issue jet. This unfortunately was not owned by the military but the PHLC. The PHLC used it to deliver supplies to different countries. This day it was being used as a cover to launch an extraction.

Catherine waited patiently. When the doors finally opened and the stairs rolled out, Gastin walked towards the stairs and looked up, bowing his head as the Supreme Chancellor walked out. From behind him, four others followed. They were not dressed as military men, but they did wear outfits that would suggest a military connection. Of the four men, two were extremely tall. The Supreme Chancellor himself was over 6-foot-4 but he seemed small in comparison. Gastin reached out his hand to the Supreme Chancellor.

"I received your message that you have some intel to share with us."

"Yes, Gastin. We have received some intel from one of our valued sources that Paxton was spotted crossing over into the U.S. and he is hiding among the soldiers headed for District 8."

Catherine paled; she could not believe they knew where Paxton was heading. The Supreme Chancellor told everyone to listen. "These four soldiers are our finest extraction team."

He lined them up and then called each one forward by name to show off their skills. The Supreme Chancellor pointed to the first man, who had a mane of glossy black hair with silver streaks along the side; he didn't look old but he had an air of danger about him.

"This is the captain of the team, Rocco Bernard."

Ethan whispered to Lars, "He does not look a match for Paxton."

Rocco started to strip down, and once he was completely naked, his bones started to break as he transformed, the cracking sound filling the air. His pale skin peeled back. It exposed a giant werewolf, completely white. The Supreme Chancellor looked on smugly. "Isn't he something? But the best part is that he is immune to silver."

This took Gloria and the others by surprise. They had heard rumors of anomalies like this but never believed

PROPHECY

it to be true. Or had the Council of Dark somehow perfected genetic tampering?

The Supreme Chancellor continued. "Rocco's father was a vampire and his mother a werewolf. This is only one of two times a union of this type was ever formed. Because of this union and its forbidden nature, Rocco is the last of his kind. They were called silverback werewolves."

Next, the Supreme Chancellor moved down the line to one of the extremely tall guards. A quick nod from the Supreme Chancellor and he began to change, his figure growing grotesque, doubling in size.

The Supreme Chancellor began talking again. "His neck is so thick that he has had three swords shatter attempting to cut off his head."

Lars was struck by this, a werewolf immune to silver and another one almost impervious to the sharpest sword. Paxton could be in trouble. They all could.

"When Brock was born, his bone structure was deformed causing it to be extra thick but when he was turned to a werewolf, the genetic mutation simply fixed the abnormalities and even thickened the strength of his structure. It is because of his bone growth that he is so large and the density makes his blows feel like a tank is hitting you."

Brock stepped back as the Supreme Chancellor called up his next soldier and introduced him. "Redfire is neither werewolf nor vampire, but one of the very few working warlocks. He was born in the 1600s and was part of a very powerful tribe of female witches. He was trained by them and discovered that he possessed an insatiable desire for more power. He found a way to harness the power from each witch, killing them one by one, eating their hearts and burning their bodies – inhaling their essence as they burned. It is those that escaped that named him Redfire. He is also the best tracker the Covenant of Dark has ever had."

Catherine swallowed hard. "I hope not," she thought, hoping that Hayden was supremely better and would reach Paxton first.

"Lastly, my son Liam, he is one of the most skilled vampires with a blade and is able to take almost anything and turn it into a weapon. He is so skilled as a marksman that he always hits his target and has never lost a sword fight before."

Lars looked at Liam with deep intensity; he felt surge of anger towards Liam. It was obvious that Liam could sense it and smiled smugly. Liam changed and rotated two long blades around his body with precision. There was no doubt that he was a master swordsman. Lars looked forward to their battle.

The Supreme Chancellor added, "I require Gastin to also accompany us on the plane, since he is now sitting on the council. I think it is time that we embarked on our journey to…catch Paxton."

Catherine hid her surprise. It was not usual but she could say nothing. She felt as if she stood on shifting sands. Life was getting dangerously out of control. There was an undercurrent and she felt that her foundations had been severed, fragmented and it was important to go with the flow. "I have selected Lars to accompany us to retrieve Paxton," she said. "He is a

PROPHECY

loyal member of the Covenant of Light and will do what he must to make sure Paxton is captured."

The Supreme Chancellor looked at Gastin and silent thoughts seemed to transfer between them. Catherine frowned. Her position was being usurped. The Supreme Chancellor looked at Catherine and nodded slowly. "Please board; we only have so much night left before daybreak is upon us."

Lars knew he had to look out for Catherine. She was his number one priority with Paxton on the run. They moved forward together, Lars flanking her side.

"There is just one more condition that I need to impress upon you." The Supreme Chancellor looked at Catherine and smiled slowly. "The Captain is in charge on this mission and all orders go through him. Can Lars honor that?"

Catherine looked at Lars and as he stepped forward, he said, "You can trust I will honor my Lord in the capture of Paxton Holt."

The Supreme Chancellor nodded. "Good, good, very good. I would hate to have Liam put a sword through your heart if you disobeyed us."

Lars knew he had to control his anger. He just bowed and took a step back.

Catherine was relieved that Lars had stepped forward. She knew this mission was not going to be easy at all and having the additional men on board was just complicating matters. Catherine turned to the Supreme Chancellor. "Can you honor one request from the daughter of Vigo?" She knew she had to use what power she had left to get what she was asking for.

"Maybe, my dear, what is your request?"

"All I ask is that we capture Paxton. I promise you as long as we don't engage him in a fight, he will not fight back. He will listen to Lars and me."

The Supreme Chancellor looked at Catherine and agreed, patting her arm. "I think we can manage that as long as he does not make the first move."

Catherine bowed, and followed him onto the plane. When they had taken their seats, the Supreme Chancellor announced, "Time to go to District 8."

* * *

I felt bleary-eyed. The TX2 had stopped again. Two more states had passed and I struggled to get my bearings. "Where are we sir?"

"We are on the fringe of District 5 and 8."

I wasn't sure how much farther I needed to go. My one advantage and disadvantage after Vigo's death was that we had traveled from the mountains back through the underground caves that led back to Canada and Safe Haven. This had kept us concealed from the outside world, unaware of all that was going on in the UDA. If they had not closed up those caves, I could have taken that route and wouldn't have had to sneak into the country masquerading as a soldier.

I looked at the surroundings outside of the TX2. It seemed as if we were going to make camp here. The officer had decided before entering the checkpoints, we would all need a good meal.

PROPHECY

"What state was this before it became a district?" I looked around feeling a slight sense of familiarity sweeping over me.

I could tell the officer was puzzled. "Soldier, this is simple geography. This was the great state of Kansas and one of the safest places to live when the bombs hit. It had no military significance and was outside of the radius."

I couldn't resist a smile, we were here. Now all I had to do was keep my soldier identity until nightfall and then sneak off. The next few hours dragged. I didn't really want to eat, but everyone else appeared to be hungry and I didn't want to stand out, so I forced myself to accept food. I had to admit, I felt a little bit better for doing so. The campfire was mesmerizing, the flames licked up the dry kindling that had been found and the heat was intense. Gradually, with a difficult day ahead of them, the soldiers started heading into the barracks. I waited patiently until the night was still. Grabbing my backpack, I made my way towards the fence perimeters but from out of the shadows I realized that someone else had been waiting patiently too.

"Where are you heading, Gomez?"

"Just want to get some fresh air, Jack."

"I said it before and I will say it again. I know you are not part of this army or any other army around here."

I fought the temptation to put him to sleep but knew that he would set off the alarm after I did so, and I had enough people chasing me. "What do you want, Jack?"

"To fight for a cause greater than me."

I had no time to waste. "If you come with me you have a good chance for a battle and an even greater chance of dying."

I hoped that this would deter the young man, but it did more to excite him. "I am in. You are going to need me, Gomez."

I sighed. His death would be on my hands. "Once we get out of here you can call me Paxton." I looked around to see if anyone else was awake…silence. It had been 200 years since I had returned to the country, maybe I could use Jack's expertise. It never hurt to have a guide, even one eager to die.

"Grab your stuff," I told him. "Stay close and quiet and whatever you see that you may find impossible, if God is my witness, if you say a word or scream. I will kill you myself."

Jack nodded. "Where are we heading?"

I looked at him; there was no sign of fear. "Scott's City, Kansas."

Chapter 13
Release the Reaper

*****

Just outside of Nebraska, the dark figure stood surrounded by a garrison of dead soldiers, their bodies flat, their heads lying away from their bodies. It was a complete massacre. The air was scented with bloodshed and the foul stench of vomit. He activated his com-link. A figure, swathed in shadows, materialized on the screen.

"Have you located him yet?"

"No master, but I know exactly where he is heading."

"You must move quickly. They are coming with an extraction team. Catherine is with them. You understand what it is you need to do?"

"I do, master."

"Has any human noticed you or can they identify you?"

The dark figure looked around, scanning bodies that covered half an acre of land. No one moved. Their severed heads told a silent story. "It is safe to say that I am in the clear."

"Good. Get to him before they arrive." His eyes glowed with pure malice. "If any of them get in your way, kill them."

The link went dark. It was time. The figure began to run straight through the discarded bodies, faster than a normal human but not as fast as a vampire or werewolf. His eyes glowed from within his hood, adding to the eerie impression. He always kept the hood in place, until the moment before he killed. This last-minute revelation ensured that the final message sent through to that individual's synapses was his face. The hooded figure stopped running after covering 10 miles in just five minutes. In supreme physical fitness, he stood, a lone figure gazing across roads in three directions. A makeshift sign pointed ahead to District 8, then District 7 to the right and District 9 to the left. The hooded figure sniffed the air, using all his senses to determine the way forward. He closed his eyes, intuitively searching for a sign. His instinct told him to go straight ahead. He set off covering large areas of ground, embracing the physical movement, heading into danger. With senses tingling, he allowed his instinct to lead him towards the ultimate confrontation. It was what he had been born for.

The extraction team landed. District 6 had cleared them to land at one of their three airstrips. They all knew their cover. They were there to deliver supplies to Districts 7 and 8. This ensured that they had complete access to all areas and would receive military cooperation. Catherine became the spokesperson, but it was Captain Bernard's plan and team to lead. The Supreme Chancellor remained on the plane. There was no doubt that they were authorized to do what was necessary to get Paxton back dead or alive. Gastin went off alone, but was advised that a separate jet would pick him up in 48 hours irrespective of the success of the mission. Each took their orders seriously. Only Catherine and Lars did not want the outcome to be the death of Paxton.

* * *

I could tell by the look on Jack's face that our exit from the barracks had been more than a little surprising. I supposed carrying him over my shoulder while I climbed indicated that I had superior strength and perhaps, was not what I seemed.

"How did you do that? Who are you?" He straightened his crumpled army jacket and looked at me in sheer wonder.

I gave Jack a look that I hoped would deter him from asking questions.

Jack held up his arms – message received loud and clear. "Okay, okay, I get it. I won't ask again."

We were now clear of scrutiny from the camp and I felt pretty certain that we would not be missed for hours. "We should be in Kansas by morning," I said, almost wistfully.

"You know Kansas well?"

"I did," I admitted. "A very long time ago." I could tell that Jack had a million questions to ask. I couldn't blame him, he had offered his services and swore allegiance to me but he didn't have a clue as to who I was.

"If you are not army and you haven't been around for some time, what have you been doing?"

I laughed. "You wouldn't believe me if I told you."

Jack smiled. "It's a good story then, I guess?"

I nodded. "My life is dangerous, Jack. It's getting more dangerous all the while. You still have time to get out of this, you know. I can't guarantee your safety, hell, I can't even guarantee mine."

"There is someone stronger than you?" He raised his eyebrows. "This is some serious…"

I cut in. "If I were you, I would get out of this now. If you stay, you will witness things that no normal man should see. The chances are that you will witness things just before you die. Unless you have a death wish…"

"I have nothing to live for," he interjected and I could tell he meant it.

"I am sorry for that," I said and I meant it. Life was for living and for making the best of the time you had. Jack seemed to be careering to an early death by choice.

"You seem older than your years. Is this through experience or…or…?"

"I knew Kansas when it was beautiful, when life was normal. Before I was told that I was chosen. Chosen to change the future."

Jack inhaled sharply. "Then you must…you must be – seriously old."

I laughed. "Yes, seriously old sums it up – thanks for that. So tell me about you?"

"I come from a long line of soldiers dating back before World War III. My family had fought in many different branches of the armed forces. When my grandfather told me stories about our history, he always referred to our family tree as being filled with agents. He always said it was a lot of cloak-and-dagger stuff. So it just stayed with me."

I nodded, absent-mindedly, guessing that Jack's family history was fueling his need to make a difference in his own right. I had always loved history, had been keen to research more of my own, until my present and future had taken a distinctly supernatural turn. Most of the remaining rogue vampires operated outside of the UDA. It was no longer this supreme power since it was in Europe that the PHLC had at least one of their two main facilities. I wondered if Jack could give me some unique insight into the area.

"So Jack, tell me more about what you know of this place we are in right now."

He reeled off facts happily. "Since we are no longer trading for materials outside of this place, the reconstruction of our country has been slow. We have spent most of it on erecting the walls around our ports. Each remaining civilian is given a job and their work is paid for in rations for their families. Everyone has a home." He stopped himself. "Mostly everyone. Not everyone has a job. The government gives two options – limited rations or if they send their husband or oldest sibling to the military they will get premium rations. Their families force most. I didn't have to but I chose to."

An emerging civilization from the ruins of a former city. I grimaced, it certainly wasn't progress. I preferred the Kansas of my youth.

Jack went on and on about the past that I had almost completely left behind. But the past was enveloping me even now – I realized I had never truly escaped its clutches. None of us had. It was encased in a poisonous new wrapper called progress and survival. Why had I chosen to go home after all of these years? It had been so long ago. Maybe for some reason I had felt that I needed some closure from my old life. Whatever the reason, I sighed, I was almost there. The day seemed long, but Jack's conversation and vast knowledge of the local history was comforting. I was content to let him talk while we walked. Within one day, we had reached our destination. I remembered it differently, but then so much had changed in the 200-plus years that I have been away.

I felt a strong sense of nostalgia and a little bit of trepidation. As we entered the town, things seemed fairly quiet. This was too strange.

"Is there a military post in this area?"

Armed men flanked our exit, materializing out of thin air seemingly. More surrounded us.

"Where is your garrison, soldiers? Where are you headed?" The soldiers had noticed the bags we carried and assumed that we had run from our duty. I could have kicked myself for not discarding the packs. It was important to talk our way out of it, but not right now. The gun was pointed right at my chest. This was one of those moments where I could easily disarm them and probably still get shot. I thought how I would explain this to the town's onlookers that had shown up to watch what was going on.

"Jack, do nothing. Let them take us," I warned.

"I am not going to rot in some military prison. I would rather go down fighting," he hissed.

I shook my head. "Trust me on this, Jack, this is the best thing we can do right now."

Jack's eyes glowed green. I could tell he was undecided. His need to go out in a burst of violent glory was strong within him.

I dropped my bag and weapons.

"What is this stick?" one of the soldiers asked.

"We have a bag of weapons; let's leave him with his little stick," another soldier said, laughing. "Take them to the cells."

Jack looked at me, confused. "I hope you are right about this."

"Believe me, I am." I placed my hands behind my back so they could cuff me. "We will only be here for one night."

* * *

Not more than several hours behind them, the dark figure made his way, stopping only to determine Paxton's direction. He could feel that Paxton was not alone. This was curious but not an issue. He looked around, able to view his surroundings even in the inky blackness. His speed was fast, close to the short-term speed of a cheetah, but he was able to sustain it for much longer. He could sense that Paxton was not far ahead of him. He licked his lips in anticipation of the battle that lay ahead.

* * *

Catherine thought about her love. She couldn't believe that things had gone so terribly wrong. How had it come to this? Paxton had done so many bad things against vampires and werewolves, but he did it only for the protection of humankind. He protected those who had fought by his side to preserve what humanity remained. Purebloods had no trace of humanity. Only those that were once humans had a faint memory of it. To them it was an unattainable dream and they were torn between it and the blood lust that came with immortality.

A voice rang out as their vehicle stopped. "Our werewolves have picked up his scent."

"Not long now then." The captain turned to Lars and said, "I thought Paxton was some great hunter? Let me guess, the legend is bigger than the man." He smirked as he walked past Lars.

Under his breath, and as faint as he could to not be heard, Lars spoke softly and with malice, "Oh Captain, you have no idea what you are getting yourself into."

* * *

In the jail cell, I sat quietly building up my energy levels for the inevitable fight to the death. The moon was full and the air was chilled, there was a tangible sense of death in the air. I had witnessed so much and yet there was still more blood to shed.

"I can't believe you talked me into surrendering. This is not how I wanted to go, rotting in some cell. I want to be out there fighting and then dying for what I believed in. Now how can I do that from behind these bars?"

PROPHECY

"Jack, can I let you in on a secret that has existed for so long?" I had his attention. "That there is a world of immortal creatures – vampires, werewolves, and witches."

"Is this a bedtime story? Something to keep me sweet?" Jack snorted. "Those stories were popular in the 21st century. We live in the real world where we have our own kind of hell."

I could hear noises in the undergrowth outside, strange noises that echoed in the darkness, a scent of anger, of blood lust and a desire to get to me. The bars at the window began to buckle, cement fragments fell like dust. Two red hairy claws began pulling at the stonework. A deformed face could be seen rising above the bricks, deep glowing eyes staring at me and through me. Within seconds, the steel frame encased within the cement wall gave way. Silence and dust filled the air. I did not move. I was ready. From out of the shadows, a figure jumped and rolled into the cell.

Jack fell back against the wall, his green eyes bulging, heart racing.

It was Hayden.

"What, what, what is that thing?" Jack croaked.

Hayden returned to his human form and gave Jack an icy stare. "You just hurt my feelings."

I laughed and Hayden joined in. Moving from my seated position, I grabbed the kill instrument.

Hayden looked at both of us. "Well, are we going to get out of here or just start cuddling?"

"Forever the joker," I smirked. "Coming?" I said to Jack. "You wanted action. Shall we go get some?"

As we walked down the dusty track roads, I holstered the kill instrument as it started to glow bright silver. "You know, Hayden, I had everything under control."

"Hmm." He coughed gently. "Sure, being locked up in a cell is one way of having things under control."

"Are you okay?" I looked at Jack. He looked pale, still shaky.

"I guess what you were saying was true then about werewolves and vampires?"

"Don't forget witches, the damned things," Hayden broke in.

"Yes," I told Jack softly. "There is a war between the good faction – the Covenant of Light and the bad faction – the Covenant of Dark. I am being hunted for a crime I did not commit."

"I came on behalf of Catherine," Hayden cut in as Jack digested this new information. "This bounty they have for you is pretty incriminating. Be straight with me. I won't care either way, but did you kill the Supreme Chancellor?"

I looked at Hayden in surprise. "I most certainly did not."

"Fine. That's what I thought, but someone is setting you up, and we have to work out why."

Jack stopped me. He looked confused. "What the hell is going on? You need to fill me in before I go any further. You really aren't kidding me about all this supernatural stuff?"

I shook my head. "Sorry, Jack. The supernatural world coincides with yours and it is more powerful than you can imagine."

He contemplated for a moment. "He's a werewolf, are you a vampire?"

"No. I am about 300 years old. I am a hunter that has fought in God's name on the side of good to keep humanity safe from vampires and werewolves."

"But you are friends with...a werewolf." Jack scratched his head. "Is that, er, normal where you come from?"

"There are those that wish to change what they are. So we have a good versus evil playing out. Luckily, you chose the good side." I paused. "You said you wanted to die for a cause, what better than for humans like yourself? This is your chance to make a difference."

Hayden touched my arm. "We have to go. They are coming."

"Who?"

"The Covenant of Dark's extraction team. They want to see justice, they said, but I don't think a court appearance is their form of justice."

"A death squad," I said, already resigned to this fact.

Hayden nodded. "I think so."

Jack concluded, with what seemed to be a reassuring gesture, "I'm with the big guy's suggestion, let's go."

Hayden smiled. "I have a classic 2175 TXR jeep 8x8, it's parked out of sight down there." He pointed to a narrow lane.

"I'm impressed." I said. "Where did you get it?"

Hayden grinned again. "Let's just say it is courtesy of District 6."

We started walking towards the vehicle.

I tried one more time to convince Jack to go. "Jack, you have every right to know what is going on and what you are up against. I am being hunted from all sides but I don't know why. If the supernatural beings don't kill me, the military will. This isn't your fight; you don't have to die today."

"I'm coming," he declared. We were at the jeep and slid into our seats as Hayden quickly started the ignition.

Hayden had secured some weapons, not ideal for killing vampires or werewolves, but something that would help fight the fight. As the jeep came to life, its engine rattled before settling, and the sound could be heard from a distance.

The jeep sped away, just as several soldiers came scurrying out of the gates, firing at Hayden and myself in the front seat. From his crouching position in the jeep Jack could hear the sound of the bullets penetrating the front window of the jeep.

"I thought this had bulletproof windows and reinforced body armor?"

"This is an oldie. She had one major flaw and that was, depending on the range and caliber of the bullet, it

PROPHECY

could penetrate. This one has likely seen way too many bullets."

Jack looked up as the moonlight glinted in through the window. "Are you hit? Hey buddy, Paxton took two bullets in the chest. We have to stop."

"We can't stop here. He will be alright."

I didn't dare straighten up. I couldn't start to heal until I got the bullets out. I ripped my shirt open. I used my knife to carve the bullets out of my chest.

"What the hell?" Jack cried. "How the hell are you not dead?"

"Just lucky I guess." I grunted as the first bullet came out. Immediately, the wound started to heal. I wiped away the blood. All that remained now was a faded scar.

"I cannot be easily killed. Once human, I am now immortal – to a point," I corrected and groaned as I tried to reach the second bullet, which was lodged under my ribs. It was affecting my breathing, having hit my rib and lungs. I extended the hole by an inch so I could slide two fingers in. Pain pierced through me and I yelled. Blood was pumping out but I was able to push the bullet forward from an angle and my fingers grabbed it and pulled it out.

"Thank God for this window." I looked at Hayden. "It would have gone right through me and possibly through Jack."

Jack looked up. "You're right. I really wouldn't want to go like that. Where's the glory?"

.Hayden looked over at me. "Heading south?"

I nodded as he turned off the track and onto the road. I could feel my lung healing and the skin puckering as it all pulled together. "Keep heading south, just on the fringe of District 8. This was once Kansas. I have somewhere I want to go."

Hayden understood all too well. "On our way."

* * *

From a distant viewpoint, the hooded figure sat in the shadows watching the jeep as it sped away. He wanted further confirmation that Paxton was still heading for his old hometown and the direction now seemed to confirm so. He jumped down from his perch, which was over 30 feet from the ground, landing nimbly on his feet. He set off at a fast pace, he didn't want to lose the jeep. He had his mission and everything was going just as planned.

* * *

"The prisoners have escaped and have made their way from the compound. We are tracking them with satellite imagery." The radio crackled as Catherine and the rest of the crew in the truck gathered all the intel as it was cascaded from the radio to the monitors. The signal was heading south.

Catherine clenched at her stomach; waves of sickness flooded her senses. Lars leaned in as the others looked over and asked her what was wrong.

"Nothing," she lied. She had taken some blood capsules. Each capsule was no larger than a normal size aspirin, but it pushed out eight ounces of blood as it came in contact with water or other fluids like saliva.

PROPHECY

Captain Bernard leaned over and said, "You had better get that under control or we will leave you at the next stop. We can't have you slowing us down."

Catherine looked up in annoyance. "I am fine." Catherine knew the baby inside of her was growing so fast. How fast she wasn't sure. At this rate, she could be giving birth at any moment. She just knew she had to get to Paxton. He had a right to know he was going to be a father. She hoped it would give him something to fight for. Lars slipped her some blood capsules and she held them in her mouth as the blood dispersed and she swallowed with great pleasure. It was enough to keep the weakness at bay.

* * *

We made it to our first stop.

"It's an old factory." Jack was puzzled.

"It's not the factory but what is underneath it that is so important," Hayden informed him.

We walked around the outskirts of the factory, where several trees still stood. Jack had a flashlight to help him pierce the darkness whereas for me, it was as if coming home. The headlights from the 8x8 all-terrain vehicle were bright and projected a glow in and around the factory. I sat down by the tree while my good friend Hayden took watch. I thought about Vladimir a lot, it may have been 235 years or so ago but to me, it felt like days. Immortality made it easy to think about things when you didn't have to worry about dying.

I closed my eyes, tuning in to the hunters before me.

Vladimir, thank you for watching out for me even after your death. I know that the voice I hear at times is yours and it has been a great comfort to me.

I paused and looked up, turning my face to the stars. I projected to the heavens without saying an actual word.

Vladimir, I wanted to come and celebrate our day. The day you saved my life and the day I became a hunter. I have tried to live each day the way you had lived yours. I have read all that you have written in the book and kept it close to me. I am sorry that it took over 200 years to come back and tell you this, but it seemed necessary to come now. I feel a great evil out there. It grows stronger each day. It is much bigger then Vigo or the Covenant of Dark. It seems as if some things change while other things remain the same. If this is the last time I will be here, where you died, I want you to know I think of you and Clay every day. I will keep fighting until my dying breath.

As I sit here I implore you to help me. I can't do this alone. If you are truly the voice I hear looking out for me send me a sign.

I pulled out a small wooden cross from my bag. It had the initials V.H. on the back. I closed my eyes and said a prayer. One day we will meet again old friend, one day.

Hayden's finely tuned senses had picked up a sound. Something approached from the north and from the northeast. I stood up, shaking off the fear as if it were dust on my shirt.

Hayden spoke softly to Jack. "Are you ready, Jack? This is the moment of truth. We have a fight on our hands. We understand if you are not with us. This fight will not be worldly."

"I am in," Jack said resolutely.

"Climb a tree and wait there but be ready to pave the way," I instructed Jack and he moved quickly to a tree with dense foliage. I could hear him scrambling up into the branches.

"Hayden, take form, we may need your full strength on this one!"

Hayden moved aggressively towards the oncoming vehicles. He took off all his clothes and began the transformation. Jack saw it all, heard the snapping of bones and noted the sudden expansion of his chest. He watched Hayden shake his body like a wet dog, each time, his bulk growing ever large. Now he was the size of a grizzly bear but red with razor-sharp teeth.

I pulled out my kill instrument and waited. Hayden knew not to attack unless given the order. I looked at the kill instrument. It was pure silver. There had to be more werewolves than vampires.

A large truck pulled up and I stood defiantly, the lights blazing a trail in the darkness. I sniffed the air, familiar scents but not all. Momentarily blinded by the lights, I could hear all of the doors opening.

"Paxton! It's me, it's Catherine."

My heart nearly leapt out of my chest. She was in my arms. Her lips were soft on mine. Her arms were wrapped around me. I breathed in her heady scent and nearly groaned in pleasure. Lars moved forward, he shook my hand. I felt touched but knew this was just the beginning.

"Paxton, I have so much to tell you, so much has changed."

I raised an eyebrow. Whatever was going on had been well planned; I just couldn't piece together the fragments of the puzzle. Catherine reached for her com-link to get Gastin on the line. As she flipped it open, the power went off. Hayden growled softly, in warning.

Captain Bernard moved forward. "I have this cool little device in my hand. It disables all devices within a 10 miles radius of our location. Now, assuming you are equipped with devices that contain a DW3 frequency chip, you are out of luck and, Paxton, well, you are out of time."

Catherine looked at the captain. "We had a deal. Paxton would come quietly and he would have a fair trial."

Captain Bernard laughed. "We were never here to bring you in. In fact, none of you are to return."

Catherine stepped forward with barely concealed aggression. "You can't do this! My father was the head of all of this. When he died I took over. I demand you put a stop to this if you know what's best for you."

Catherine's eye started to glow as the power shimmered through her and exploded in a second like a burnt-out flame. She staggered and then collapsed. I caught her before she hit the ground.

"What's wrong with her?" I gasped.

"The baby inside of her is draining her strength," Captain Bernard acknowledged. "Yes, Catherine, the council has been aware of your pregnancy – probably long before you. We cannot let this child be born. We have to stop the prophecy from coming true. You will all suffer a true death."

The words from Captain Bernard cut into my chest like a dual blade. The fire within me started to burn and I could feel the darkness in me rise up like a serpent out of the ground. I wanted to strike hard and fast at that moment, but then a voice came over me. A baby. I could feel the serpent slowly retracting back into the hole. A baby? My baby. I am going to be a father. The darkness came back again and this time it spoke with a snake's tongue. "Not if you don't finish this fight now." Something approached and I had regained my conscious self.

Another vehicle had pulled up. The four of us were now outnumbered.

"I will make a deal with you, Paxton," the captain said. "If you give us your life, I will let the others live. What do you say? Your life for theirs?"

Catherine whimpered. "No, Paxton. He will kill us anyway."

"Hayden," I said, "take Catherine and do not let anyone within 10 feet of her."

The impressive form swept Catherine up in his arms and headed to the tree where Jack was perched. Jack looked through the scope as I nodded my head.

Jack pointed the scope at Captain Bernard, and squeezed the trigger. "Liam!" the captain cried out. The shot was dead on, but as if in slow motion, Liam's sword came up towards Captain Bernard's face, cutting the bullet in half, as both halves passed by the captain's head, leaving small singe marks in his hair.

"So I guess I have your answer. I hoped you could have saved your friends." The Captain ordered the other men from the recently arrived convoy to stay back as he wanted a piece of the great Paxton Holt.

I looked at Lars, his swords drawn, his gaze loyal. "Like old times," I said. We clasped arms. "To the end."

"It is time that I prove to my father that I am truly the world's best swordsman," Liam Vega cried.

Lars merely positioned himself, anticipating any move. He had spent over 200 years with me, who lived by my sense of humor, and he said something to make me proud. "I am sorry you have some repressed daddy issues but don't you worry, my therapy offers a swift and bloody solution." Lars merely smirked, noting that he had indeed hit a raw nerve.

"You will pay dearly for that. I will make sure I kill you limb by limb. Nice and slowly." Liam surged forward, his eyes blazing.

"Liam, Brock, Redfire, kill Hayden and that bitch Catherine and her unborn abomination," the Captain shouted.

Hayden was ready as the two werewolves met head to head, but with the first blow, he was driven back. Hayden was big but the werewolf known as Brock was even bigger and his blow on Hayden was like nothing he had ever felt. Each blow was made with steel. Hayden recovered his poise as the two circled each other, just growling and sizing up their next move. Hayden knew he was outsized but had to find a weakness and quickly.

I was very aware of the battle going on around me but I had my own problems going fist to fist with the Captain and Redfire. It might have looked like an old-time brawl but with three supernatural beings. I blocked each blow from the Captain and countered, at the same time, dueling magic with Redfire. We sent different spells back and forth, attack and defense. I was glad I had practiced fighting and spell craft. Between us, we created a wondrous light show with deadly consequences. I spun out of the way of an oncoming spell, spiraling into a move that sent the Captain flying and crashing into a nearby tree. I could hear Jack firing at will and hoped that some of the bullets hit their moving targets.

Jack aimed at Redfire, grazing his shoulder. This gave me the opportunity to dive in and help Hayden. My old friend was bleeding. His red fur was made darker by the blood that flowed down from his shoulder. Brock was strong, but most of all extremely dense physically. This made Hayden's strike less impactful on Brock. As Brock was about to go back for another piece of Hayden, I lowered my shoulder and altered Brock's course just enough for Hayden to get to his neck and to draw blood himself. This did not overly stun Brock as he used his back legs to kick out at me, catching me in the pit of my stomach. He then threw Hayden to the side. Winded, I looked up, realizing that Catherine was vulnerable and Brock was heading straight for her.

I blinked as a hooded figure materialized and drew his swords, slashing at Brock's neck. Blood splattered an angry trail around and Brock snarling immediately turned his attention on the new player. I didn't know who he was but it bought me some much needed time and I went after Redfire while Hayden charged at the Captain.

The battle seemed to ensue forever. The Captain called in the reinforcements. I could see that we needed to end this battle quickly before being overwhelmed by more. This battle was getting ever more deadly. Jack had dropped down from the tree and was protecting Catherine, firing at all those who were heading their way, in human form and werewolves.

* * *

The hooded figure was becoming bored with the fight. It was an unnecessary waste of energy and was complicating his mission. As Brock lunged for the hooded figure, he flipped lithely out of the way and then whispered a strange incantation over and over as Brock froze in midair. Only his eyes could move and they bulged with unknown fear. The hooded figure pulled out another sword and stood over Brock's head as his werewolf eyes watched. He could see the face of the figure under the hood and his eyes widened yet further. The hooded figure had both swords up over his head, he saw his moment and with all his power, he came down with the swords. As the blades met each other, they sparked and then the head rolled forward. Brock was no more.

***

I turned, witnessing Brock's head rolling across the ground. The hooded figure, ninja-like and deadly, raised two bloodied swords in the air. A bullet whistled past my head and found its target. Jack had spotted a soldier attacking me from behind. This slowed the man down as the bullet shattered his shoulder, and lined him up perfectly for me to pull out the kill instrument and to slam it through the soldier's heart. Jack watched, mesmerized. Catherine had regained some energy and leapt to her feet, defending Jack, biting down on the werewolves that approached. Jack staggered back out of the way, watching as Catherine semi-changed, drained the werewolf, dropping him to the floor and biting the other one too. She sucked on his neck until his legs and arms stopped moving. Her eyes and body had changed; she looked demonic, half-crazed, attacking the soldiers who had not changed form. She drained all of them. The baby's thirst for blood was unquenchable.

Liam was pushing Lars back. But facing the barrage of blows was merely sapping him of his strength. It seemed as if Liam was getting the upper hand on him. He slashed at his arms and face, just missing cutting through the neck on several swings. Blood flowed from Lars' face and he felt his immortality slipping. He was doing just enough to defend Liam's strikes but had nothing to counterattack. Then it dawned on him that Liam was opening up his hips during his offensive strikes. This was so that he could put more power in his downward strikes. The speed had obscured his vision and ability to anticipate. He had more than likely finished off most of his opponents quickly so they never had the time to see this flaw in his defense. The one problem Lars had was if he didn't plan it at the right time, he would be decapitated in the process.

Liam kept up his attack, sensing that Lars was slowing down. As he came forward, he went into a spin-out from Lars striking at the hilt of the sword. Liam's blade perfectly grazed the handle but hit its mark. This allowed Lars an even swing and to recover from side attacks more quickly, but on this occasion it was a devastating blow. Lars, who was right-handed from birth and had trained with both, found that using double hands on his sword increased his strength substantially. This move made him change his stance when he connected and he had to alter his grip to one hand, as Liam still held his sword with both. Lars could not trust both hands anymore if it did not make Liam change his grip and it also left his secret attack in question.

Liam smiled. "I will give you this, Lars, you have great skills but you are no match for me. It is time for you to die."

Lars had no angle nor any conceivable openings and only one hand truly left; he vowed to not go easily. He came in and started to attack as Liam was on the defensive, but Liam overpowered him, causing him to collapse to the ground, still with his sword in his left hand and the other hand helping him regain his balance. Lars took up a defensive guard even from the ground, but it only had a 50/50 chance of keeping him alive. Then, the opening he was looking for materialized. Jack had fired several shots at Liam, right before Jack was mauled and thrown by one of the werewolves. Jack's body hit the nearest tree causing his spine to be crushed at his lowest vertebras. He hit the ground and gasped for air as blood poured from his mouth. Jack trembled and then lay still with his eyes glazed, looking forward.

From the other side, bullets were fired in Liam's direction; he instinctively turned to counter the hail of bullets, knowing he did not have enough time to finish Lars off at that moment. He turned and used his sword finely, cutting both bullets in half. At that moment, Lars regained his balance, placing both hands on the sword, blood pooling from the open fingers. Liam turned to come down with a strike to finish him off. As he swung, all in one motion Lars spun out and took off Liam's leg. As Liam fell forwards, his face frozen with shock, Lars took off his head knowing that if it had not been for Jack, he would be dead. As grateful as he was, Lars felt that he had dishonored Liam, because he hadn't managed to beat him on his own. Jack had made it possible with his split-second opening.

Catherine came over to Lars helping him to stand and to then walk over to the bushes where she laid him down flat. He was badly injured. Lars slipped in and out of consciousness. "I have to get up and help Paxton," he murmured.

"You can't, just lie down and don't try to move." Catherine looked at him with deep compassion. "There is nothing left for you to do. Just lay still and let your wounds heal." Lars slipped back into an unconscious sleep.

Catherine wanted to check on Jack but she couldn't leave Lars. She knew that no human could have survived that trauma. She stood over Lars, watching as his body healed. She looked back; healing was slow, very slow. She couldn't explain why but then it hit her.

He had lost so much blood from having his fingers severed and a sword pushed through his chest. This was not the time to try to get blood from one of the fighting soldiers. Catherine saw what was left of one of the other soldiers and dragged his dead body over to Lars. She began to suck the blood out of his neck. The blood almost tasted like sour milk, but she knew it was still warm and Lars needed it or he would not recover soon enough. She could feel her own strength wavering.

* * *

Still immersed in the action, the hooded figure fought his way towards Catherine, slicing through anything that stood in his way. He was so smooth with his blade and gun that each movement seemed perfectly orchestrated. He kept the soldiers off balance, his calmness and fearlessness at the battle scene unnerving.

* * *

Thankful for my hunter's strength, I carried on in the battle against the Captain and Redfire. My strength was weakening though. The constant stress of fighting magic and blocking the Captain was draining. I focused on the purest thought known to man, that of my unborn child and the intensity of my love for Catherine. I had to win this battle. I had never envisaged actually becoming a father even though it had been foretold, and I didn't want to lose that opportunity now. A blade slashed a piece of my hair that was hanging in front of my face. Stay focused, I reminded myself.

It was a joint operation. Redfire constantly cast dangerous spells in my direction, making me think and taking away the effectiveness of my fighting skills. It was working too. The Captain backed off momentarily

PROPHECY

but I guessed this was a ploy. Redfire's spells mingled with dark magic was incredibly strong. My magic was pure and I felt that we were fairly evenly matched. One on one, it would be possible to take him but I couldn't stop my focus on the Captain. Out of the corner of my eye, I spotted him changing into a giant silver wolf and felt myself groan. I sent a silent message to all the hunters who had gone before me. I needed help and I needed it fast. In an instant, a plan began to form in my mind.

Just as the Captain came at me from behind, I waited until I could smell his snarling breath close to me before casting a spell that uprooted the dirt from the ground; it spiraled up blinding Redfire just long enough for me to unholster the kill instrument. I pushed the kill instrument up through the Captain's ribs and close to his heart. He fell on top of me, his teeth snapping into my neck. I pushed hard and rolled to one side as Redfire tried to send a powerful energy wave in my direction. It hit the Captain instead, burning his body. The bite had gone into my neck and shoulder, cutting deep within the muscles, I was losing too much blood and there was a great deal of damage to the shoulder area. The fall had crushed my sword arm. I felt strangely weak as toxins from the bite tried to enter my bloodstream. I knew my body was fighting to heal but I still had Redfire to deal with.

Redfire was now pulling lightning from the sky and projecting it through his hands. As it surged towards me, I cast a spell to ground the energy bolt and to send it hurtling into the soil but my magic didn't deflect it enough; the lightning hit both me and the ground in front of me. The force was enough to send me back 20 feet and down a hill, rolling between the trees. I knew that Redfire would not give up, but I did not know if he would come after me or Catherine. His mission was to kill all of us but I hoped that he would see me as the bigger prize.

I was wrong. Redfire saw his opportunity and headed straight for Catherine. He barked out orders for a few of the remaining soldiers to help him with her. Catherine stumbled to her feet, her eyes turning a dark red. The veins in her neck started to show as she tried to change, but she could not summon the energy to do so. Redfire started to chant a spell, his eyes glazed over as he summoned his inner energy, connecting with the powers of the universe. The skies darkened even more as the clouds above swirled. Lighting struck a nearby tree. His eyes and mouth were emitting a bright golden glow. His voice rang out but the sound was from all around.

"Catherine, it is time that you and that abomination growing inside of you are destroyed. There is no other way. This child is a danger to us all. It has been foreseen."

* * *

The hooded figure had just moments before Catherine was destroyed along with her unborn baby. He reached out to the soldiers surrounding him, utilizing his own magic, sending out a powerful hallucinogenic spell. The soldiers started to fall to the ground screaming, oblivious to the real danger that was approaching them. He made his way through them, slicing their heads from their bodies with amazing speed and accuracy. Just before the final blow was struck Redfire did not see or hear the tornado that was the hooded figure approaching, until it was too late. As he turned, flesh was met by steel.

He stood his ground, glowing intensely as the hooded figure waited menacingly, before slicing through the energy field. As Redfire attempted to look at the hooded figure, a determined slice to his neck ensured that his head rolled off cleanly, the power inside of him bursting out of his body up into the heavens. His headless body levitated until all the magic was gone, and then he dropped from a great height. The sky crackled, was bright for a moment and then darkness flooded the area again.

The hooded figure stood over Catherine who was in great pain. She clutched her stomach as the baby moved within. Catherine was scared that the baby was injured and there was nothing that she could do.

"My master can save you and your child. You have a choice, either you come with me now or you and your friends all die," the hooded figure told her.

Catherine had no choice. Paxton couldn't save her. Lars was not healed, and she had to save them and her baby if she could. "So, if I agree to come with you, I have your word that you will not hurt them?"

"You have my word."

"Then I will come," Catherine voiced, and in an instant, they had disappeared.

I clawed my way back up the hill, strength almost depleted. "What happened?"

Hayden was making his way back to the center of the action. He was covered with scratches, bite marks and dripping in blood. He stopped in his tracks. Dozens upon dozens of decapitated bodies sprawled all over the expanse greeted us both. It was a bloodbath. He looked as confused as me.

"Catherine? Catherine?" My stomach lurched. I couldn't bear it if she were dead. How could I look upon the dead face of my beautiful woman? I noticed Lars moving, slowly, but in pain. He was healing. He had given his all in the fight.

Lars struggled to sit up. "The hooded figure took her. They are gone."

"Was she hurt?" I needed to know but I was terrified to know the truth.

"No, he promised to spare us if she went with him. She was in a great deal of pain. He said his master could save her and the child."

"I have to go after her." I sprang to my feet, but I didn't even know where to start. As I turned round helplessly looking for some clue, I saw the naked and very much alive body of Captain Bernard.

He pulled the kill instrument out of his chest and I watched as the hole started to close up. The smell of burning flesh was obvious from the hand that held the kill instrument. His lean body seemed to be unfazed by the instrument that usually brought death in an instant.

"Did you think that this weapon of yours would kill me? I am immune to silver. I am a hybrid, half werewolf and half vampire. It takes much more than a magical stick to kill me."

PROPHECY

I could feel my anger welling up inside of me. It was their stupid plan to kill me or take me in without a trial that had caused all of this to happen. I wanted to lash out and kill him, snap his paltry neck, and scatter his bones. Hybrid or not.

"You know we were going to kill you, all especially that hot whore of yours." The Captain was taunting me. I wanted to avenge her honor.

"Let's finish this, you and me right here, right now." He spat at me. "Have your men stand back. But know this, when I am done killing you, I will find your whore and that baby and will kill them both slowly. I will cut the child from her lifeless body and I may feast on it as it breathes its first or last breath. Or I may cook it in your honor." The captain laughed, then moved closer to me as the red mists of my anger started to cloud my vision.

I wanted to erupt, my power was regenerating, but it had not broken through the surface yet. I need to finish him quickly, I thought, so I could save Catherine. Then it happened, the switch clicked to on and my inner volcano erupted.

"Paxton, maybe I will have my way with her and make her my slave after I kill your child. I always wanted a pet vampire."

I could feel my eyes turning red; it was as if they were boiling. This had never happened to me before. The voice inside me grew louder. I couldn't ignore it. I could see that he was brandishing a sword but I did not care. He went to strike me but in that instant, I used an incantation that lifted the Captain up into the air. He was powerless to fight back. I took my other hand up into the air and made a fist. I could hear the Captain's rib bones breaking. I had done this before but had forgotten how, yet as the darkness rose within me, this inner power surged. The captain started to choke as I started to squeeze with my other hand. We were only about 12 inches apart. I could hear every bone crack and splinter and the sound was music to my ears. He was screaming and I wanted more.

"I will always find a way to dismantle and destroy evil, no matter who or what you are," I cried. I pulled my hands together and then thrust my arms out wide in an aggressive movement. The Captain's body was ripped completely in half. I smiled. Catherine and the baby had one less enemy. Hayden ran towards me, and I felt the urge to attack him. But I staggered back, bloodied by the Captain's innards that had exploded around me, and fell to my knees, my head in my hands.

"I am so sorry, my friend. I don't know what got into me, one moment I am ready to fight the Captain and the next moment, I am ready to take on the world."

Hayden grabbed me. "We will find her."

I was glad of his strength and his conviction. "We don't know where she is."

Hayden's brow furrowed. "Don't be too sure of that. Catherine had a feeling that things would go south and she set up several contingency plans. We planted a tracker. Also, we have a plane not too far from this location."

I felt a surge of hope welling up inside of me.

"She wasn't all that sure what airport would still be open but she used her last connections to pull that off.

After all, the Dark Covenant would pull their privileges if she were being set up."

"I want to go now to get her. We don't know what they are doing to her." I picked up the kill instrument and holstered it. "I will get Lars into that truck, you check for survivors. We burn the dead. We can't leave any evidence of what happened here."

Lars was healing slowly but I doubted he would be able to fight anytime soon unless some miracle occurred. I carried him to the truck and placed him gently in the back. On this very day, on this night, nearly 220 years ago, a great battle took place and a young boy's destiny was changed forever. It was on that day that it became clear to me that there was a great evil out there and that someone had to bring it down. I could see Hayden was busy burning all of the bodies. I felt sad. It needn't have happened. None of it.

I thought about Vladimir and how I had promised to burn his body. I will see you soon, old man. How soon is all in my own hands.

"Did you see Jack?" I asked Hayden, fearing the worst.

"Yes," he said simply. "He died fighting a good cause. He saved Lars."

I felt a sense of sadness for the man who had willingly given his life. At least he had died fighting and I would never forget him. As long as I drew breath, I would honor this man who had died protecting us all. We clambered into the truck and Hayden drove. We were on our way to the airport and I just hoped we could find Catherine and I could beat the bastards who had taken her.

Chapter 14
The First Stand

*****

We ran through the trees towards the top of the hill that overlooked the castle. With the fog being so dense, it provided an ample amount of camouflage to conceal us both. Before reaching the peak of the hill, I contacted Gloria, knowing that she was waiting and would be worried.

Gloria's voice came over the com-link. "Are you guys in place?"

"We are. Bring on the noise!" Lars had followed me up to the top of the hill. We needed to get into the best position for our attack. He had recovered from his injuries in the time that it had taken for us to track Catherine down. I couldn't tell what had helped most with his recovery – his natural ability to heal, the magic incantations that I sent surging through him, or just his dogged and bloody-minded determination to rescue Catherine.

Right before the castle came into view, the rain started to fall. Thunder followed, with sparks of lightning. The sky was lit up dramatically and then blackness claimed the area. It was the lightning that revealed the figure standing at the top.

PROPHECY

Lars called to me with concern in his voice. "It's the hooded figure again?"

I felt a cold shiver go up my spine. He stood in front of me, two swords drawn in his hands ready for battle.

"I only want Paxton. You are free to go; I will not extend another offer. If you stay you will die."

I wasn't going to get Lars injured. The element of surprise had been turned on its head and Lars was not fully recovered. I knew that even if Lars would not admit to it.

"Lars, go meet up with Gloria, help her, I will face him on my own."

Lars looked at me in disbelief. "We are in this together for better or worse. I have sworn an oath to protect you and protect you I shall."

I shook my head but I also knew that stubborn tilt to Lars jaw. He wasn't going to go anywhere. I nodded my acceptance. The rain was coming down even harder in torrents, and the fog floated around the hooded figure, adding more to the sense of mystery. This was not a good day to die.

The hooded figure reached behind his back to pull out two Japanese katana samurai swords. They looked identical and even through the rain, the master craftsmanship was evident. I drew my own sword, which was said to have been forged by one of the greatest metallurgists of all time, Honjo Masamune. The sword is known as tachi. It was passed down from Lars to me. It was once the sword used by the hunter William Stanton. Where he acquired it is unknown.

Lars' sword was said to have been used by Miyamoto Musashi, one of the greatest samurais of all time. He, just as Lars, was known for his mastery of the katana.

With the rain steadily increasing, along with the battle that was taking place down below, we both knew that we were entering our next and potentially final battle. The hooded figure sensed my anticipation, so he took the initiative and within seconds, was in the air flipping towards our position. We ducked, weaved, and rolled, outmaneuvering the dual swords of the hooded figure. Each strike between the three of us sent up giant sparks. Our motions were fluid. Lars felt the blade just nick his face, he flicked his head back and the blade went past.

It was easy to see that our opponent defended effortlessly. He was lithe, nimble, flexible, and very strong. He was a supreme fighting machine. Lars and I had been practicing together for a long time, so with our familiarity, we attacked and counterattacked working as one.

It was becoming obvious that we were gaining control, besting his attacks and almost getting through his defenses. One attack came so close to taking off his leg that the leather on his boot was cut clean through, but missed any flesh. I cursed. I wanted to wrap up this dramatic scene and to find Catherine. He jumped up, missing a strike. I lunged again. As he flipped, he sent forth an incantation that picked me up and threw me 60 feet away against a giant rock. I felt the rock rough against my skin as I slid down towards the ground. My head felt as if it had exploded. I gave into the sensation and lost consciousness.

***

Lars took his eyes off the fight for a second, jumping back, needing to see if Paxton was alright. He countered, defending, and could see that his friend was out for the count. He had moved, though, so Paxton was not dead. Lars jumped back into action with renewed vigor. Both men countered each other's move, going back and forth between defense and attack. They moved so fast that no mortal would even see this mastery, it was like pure art.

***

Gloria, Hayden, Ethan, and the other soldiers from Safe Haven were in a dogfight of their own. They had caused the distraction and as a reward, vampires and werewolves poured out of the castle towards them. Some fully transformed, some partially formed, and some not at all. Both sides came to blows just inside of the immediate perimeter of the castle. Both sides pitted werewolves against werewolves, vampires against vampires, and vampires against werewolves. It was an all-out war. The enemy outnumbered Gloria's forces two to one, but what they lacked in numbers, they gained in age, experience, and strength.

Many of those fighting were young and most of them were half-bloods. Very few were purebloods. It seemed that this army had been created within the last few hundred years. Many of the werewolves were small but the numbers made the fight even. Including the vampires, they had several purebloods that fought. One in particular was very large and increasing his body count quickly. He was huge for a vampire, possessing incredible strength and even the strength of some of the other purebloods was no match for him.

Ethan fully transformed. His body size increased in every dimension. As a man he stood around 6 feet and weighed a slender 165 pounds, but as a vampire he was over 7 feet tall and his weight was based on the density of his muscles and bone structure, which had to put him around 400 or 500 pounds. He was massive. The other vampire noticed Ethan, recognizing him as the main threat, and came at him. Their battle became a show of pure strength as both vampires used their claws to go at each other. Each delivered blow after blow, but even with those strikes, neither slowed down.

Ethan tried to get his giant arms around the neck of the other vampire, searching for the right grip so that he could snap his neck and just finish off this battle. But the vampire was too smart. He saw the strength of Ethan and did not let him get too close. He tried to utilize Ethan's youth and strength against him.

As Ethan rushed in, trying to stun the other vampire, Ethan found this approach turned against him, as the vampire used Ethan's momentum, throwing him into a solid brick wall. Ethan was stunned momentarily, and cursed his stupidity. He regained his composure but now the vampire was nowhere to be seen. As Ethan pushed away from the wall, the other vampire, clutching the wall above Ethan, prepared to jump, clawing at Ethan's back and biting his neck.

Before the vampire jumped, Ethan caught a glimpse of a shadow in the dark from the moonlight. He didn't hear the vampire coming but knew that he had the upper hand. The vampire leaped at him, and he spiraled around, with his giant arms, Ethan used his weight to flip the vampire over his back. In a split second Ethan looked up, checking his safety as he came down on top of the vampire, crushing him to the floor.

Ethan became part of the action. Not a spectator but intrinsically involved. It felt as if he were a part of an old black-and-white film. He half-expected the audience to applaud. This triggered a moment from his past, the death of his parents. His adrenaline and strength increased twofold. The most noticeable change was his eyes, which turned from their normal deep red to blue. Ethan could not explain or control the changes.

Ethan thought about his parents one last time as he released the rage from within him. He looked down as the vampire used his brute strength to get up. But this last bit of effort was futile. Ethan was ready to release the rage and he did. He took his claws on his right hand and drove it through the vampire's rib cage, ripping out his heart. Instead of just crushing it, he drained it of all its blood, tossing it aside as soon as he was done. From there, with his rage still flowing like a bloodied river, he stepped on the vampire's head as if it were a bug. He relished the sound of the bones snapping, crunching. Ethan jumped up, attacking all the other forces around him. Ripping and decapitating them at the same time, he seemed oblivious to the sound of bullets. Gloria ordered the troops to push forward following the path of destruction caused by Ethan.

While pushing forward, Gloria did not see that some of the vampires and werewolves were hiding within their own group. They lunged for her, aiming for her neck. A werewolf was coming in to finish the job, but Giovanni noticed that Gloria was in danger and he swooped, decapitating the vampire with a solid blow. Unfortunately, the werewolf was able to get ahold of him before he could transform. In these final moments, Gloria and Giovanni locked eyes. Time stood still. Giovanni accepted his fate. He would die protecting Gloria and it was how it should be. Gloria was too weak as she tried to transform to speed up the healing process and to get to Giovanni. In those final seconds, Giovanni was able to grab his sword and thrust it through the werewolf's head just as the slavering teeth bit down and sliced him in half.

The murder of her friend ignited the animal in Gloria. She went over to Giovanni, noting his expression. There was no fear, merely determination. Gloria took the sword and with every ounce of energy, decapitated the werewolf. As it changed back, she noticed a tattoo on the left shoulder. It was one she had seen before and the same one seen during Paxton's debriefing of the ambush in Africa. It was the symbol of the Children of Judas. This symbol of the occult had been around for as long as she could remember. The symbol was a circular spiral and in the middle of the circle an infinity symbol formed. Gloria recalled that she had been told that it meant there was truly no ending.

Gloria looked down at Giovanni and leaned forward, closing his eyes. "Sleep, my brother, for you are now with our father. May I have the strength to help Paxton and the others end this war once and for all."

Gloria stood up and rejoined the fight. She was weak, but her wounds were healing.

PROPHECY

*　*　*

Now fully engaged in a battle for supremacy, Lars and the hooded figure still traded blows. I was almost to my knees, conscious now but groggy still from the impact on the rocks. I knew I had to join the fight, but found it difficult to even lift my sword. It looked as if the sheer force of my hitting the rocks had fractured my arm. The bone was clearly visible above my elbow, sticking out right through the skin. I had to reset the bone, put it back into place. Then it would not take too long for my body to heal fast. I lunged against the rocks and felt the bone click back into place. Now I could try to accelerate the healing process properly.

Watching the fight, I knew that Lars needed to try to finish off the hooded figure soon. I was stunned by the caliber of both fighters, it was almost scripted, their movements evenly matched; even so, I had the feeling that the hooded figure was toying with him, using each powerful and deadly move as a training exercise.

Lars had grown tired of this fight and had learned enough in these past minutes that he felt would lead him to victory. As he attacked, he pushed the hooded figure back. It was at this moment that Lars was able to breach his opponent's defenses. He struck his arm with a slicing motion and then slashed at the leg. This forced his opponent down onto one knee. From my vantage point, I could see Lars was moving towards victory, it was tantalizingly close. Lars had seen this moment a thousand times. It was the absolute checkmate against all of the werewolves and vampires he had faced. He deflected a defensive move, and Lars sliced the sword through his heart, finishing the fight with a clean cut of the head. Lars brought up his sword at great speed and the sword pierced through the hooded cloak.

The cloak fell harmlessly to the ground. He had disappeared. I tried to focus but the fog was obscuring my vision. It rolled across the hills, taunting me with its almost mystical presence. Lars' body was facing in my direction. He looked confused. I began to clamber up the hill, pulling myself up each craggy nook, desperate to get back to Lars and for us to work together defeating this evil.

My arm was almost healed. I could feel my restorative powers surging through me. I used my anger to accelerate the process. It was easy to tap into my inner rage at the moment, it surged through me and I knew it would until I could finally rescue Catherine. The rain was coming down harder now and the blood from my face and from my arm was pooling beneath me. I looked up at the precipice where Lars had been fighting. I couldn't see him.

"Lars?" I called to him, hoping to hear a triumphant reply but it was only the sound of rain on pitted stone that was present. The mist hung low over the rocks and I cursed the lack of visibility. I stood, uncertain, blinded by winds and a cloying fog that separated me from my adversary. I could sense danger was near though. This grey cloak around me dulled the sounds but somewhere, danger lurked. A flash of blade plunged down and I was immediately covered with red sticky blood, it splattered everywhere. I fell back, panicking, not sure where or whether I was hurt, one foot hit something on the ground and I stumbled, hitting the rocks around me heavily. A body lay with me. Broken, bloody, and yet all too familiar. His body was still warm. As the fog lifted momentarily, I saw Lars' decapitated head and his eyes, unstaring, not far from me. I felt a cold chill run through me in spite of the warmth of my exertions.

Anger boiled up in an instant. Darkness bubbled in, sending torrents of rage inwards. I wanted to curse God for letting this happen to Lars. I wanted to find his killer and to grind him into the ground, severing his head once and for all. My anger was fueling the weather, darker clouds were scurrying across the sky, lightning lit up the heavens as thunder growled its way across the region.

I was no longer afraid. I had the purpose of revenge and there was no greater intent than that. I reached down to the body of my friend and extracted the sword from his hand.

"You were my brother to the end and your life will always be remembered." I could feel the dark energy inside me, pushing the light away from my heart. It was consuming me like a cancer. I wondered if I would lose myself this night. Grief would overcome me and there would be nothing left of the old Paxton. Was this my destiny? To be lost and wandering with only rage in my heart? If I lost Catherine too, then I was nothing.

The mists were disorientating. I was sure that I could hear a woman's voice breaking through the chilled air. I assumed a defensive stance. More sorcery?

"Revenge is not the answer but redemption. Avenge your fallen friend. The dark side is in all of us, but we chose how much of it controls us."

I caught a glimpse of a woman standing, her arms upraised, her voice haunting. I picked my way over the rocks but she was gone. I doubted that she had ever been there. Ghosts were haunting me or warning me. I knew I had to focus, keep my quest firmly in my mind. I also knew that I would have to fight like never before. I began walking towards the edge of the hill as torches near the ground lit up with each step I took towards the castle. So much for the element of surprise.

Gargoyles adorned the wall high above me. They didn't move, they just watched, like silent sentries as I approached. Their eyes glowed, fueled by magic, but these guardians remained rock-like and silent. I looked along the wall to locate an entrance, there didn't seem to be any way inside. I wasn't going to give up though. I looked again; something didn't seem quite right along the wall. I closed my eyes, pressing my hands upon the stonework, feeling the history of this place pulsing underneath my battle-scarred hands. I needed to reveal its secrets. I moved along the wall, as if guided by unseen voices whispering to me.

With my eyes closed I felt my way, keeping my body flat against the wall. The stones were heating up against my torso; I could feel the warmth seeping through my clothes. Then I found it, my hands went through the wall. Even with my eyes open, I could not see the entrance but my hands were on the other side. I had found the entrance, though it was hidden by magical means. With a deep breath, I walked through.

I holstered the sword that I had taken from Lars and instead pulled out my Glock and the kill instrument. It was acting strangely. It was neither silver nor oak, but shimmered with a distinct form of red and black. I shrugged; maybe the magic surrounding the place was affecting it. I didn't care, as long as it killed when I needed it to.

Chapter 15
Judgment

*****

I walked down the long hallway, flickering torchlight heralding my way forward. It was damp, oppressive and the walls on either side felt as if they were closing in on me. I was ready for anything that might attack. The torches ahead of me began to flicker and die and part of the hallway plunged into darkness. I waited, my breath bated. Nothing happened. A room at the end lit up and I wondered if my reception party were hiding in the shadows or awaiting me in the room at the end. The room was certainly prepared for something. Illuminated by the candles on the chandelier above, adorned with a mass of crystals, prisms of light shone around the room giving a dappled and mystical appearance. I could see two closed doors within the room as I crept closer, with just a glint of surreal light showing through.

I moved forward carefully, creeping out of the shadows but stopped as something moved within the room. It was all too easy. No doubt a trap. I approached the doorway, there appeared to be nothing there, but my hunter senses prickled. I clamped my jaw shut, ready to defend against an attack. A movement again, barely visible, just out of the corner of my eye, but there all the same. It did not come at me but ran across the room so fast, that I had no chance of making out the form. I heard the grating in the lock as the door opposite me opened. I guessed I was meant to follow.

I walked stealthily, the room behind me darkened, and I headed for the light from the new room. As I walked through, I could hear scuttling noises and see doorways at the end leading to hallways and beyond. Darkness provided a screen of risk. I was sure that I was being watched. Every fiber of my being alerted me to danger. It seemed to be safe at the moment, but I decided not to provoke whatever it was that was hiding in here.

I walked further into the room, realizing that part of it had been screened from me, hidden by some magical incantation. My realization seemed to be the key to unravel the magic and my heart both leapt and sank as I realized that Catherine and Gastin were shackled together. I moved forward cautiously. They were alive at least but for how long? I studied the bonds, there seemed to be no way to break them. They looked desperate and traumatized.

"Paxton," Catherine whispered, "get out of here. Go."

My heart broke seeing her look so pale and so lacking in energy.

Gastin spoke to me, raising his shackled wrists. "Paxton, they are bound by magic. The hooded figure did this to us, can you free us?"

I pulled helplessly at the shackles; it wasn't going to be so easy to break them. "Are you both okay?" I cast a worried glance at Catherine and then Gastin.

Catherine nodded but it was Gastin who broke the tension. "The last thing I remember was getting on the plane with the council and then waking up in a cell that subdued my ability to transform. I have been unable to break out of the cell and escape."

"They have used magic – dark magic," I told him. "But I'll find a way." I looked at Catherine. She looked so frail but when I looked in her eyes, I saw that her inner spirit was strong. I leaned in for a kiss, feeling the softness of her lips, the familiar scent and taste. I renewed my resolve to save her.

"I am so sorry, Paxton," Catherine said, "I did not want this to happen. I have been so distant from you these last six months and our baby…"

"Sssh," I put one finger over her mouth, "let's get out of this place and you can apologize and make it up to me all you like." I gave her a wink, trying to sound positive but inside, I was trembling. Terrified that I couldn't save her.

I concentrated on the shackles again, chanting a few spells that my former friend Nina had told me. The chains wobbled but did not break. I pulled out the kill instrument and tried to use it to break the chains. Even with my strength and the power of the kill instrument, the chains remained strong.

"You will never break that spell! It came into being well before your time and it will outlast you."

I turned my stance defensive. One of the walls shimmered and became transparent in front of me. I guessed I had been watched from the moment I entered the room. I began to feel like some lab rat, providing

PROPHECY

information to those who had set up the experiment. Giant gossamer curtains were pulled back to reveal a stage. My eyes focused with loathing upon the hooded figure and then to a giant figure, sitting on a throne made of bones.

The man stood up and I took measure of his great height. Impressive, yet his body did not look so strong. The hooded figure also moved towards me. I pulled out the sword ready; nothing would please me more than to kill him with Lars' weapon. I reached down for the kill instrument too and then prepared myself for battle.

The man standing by his throne clapped slowly. "Very nice form, impressive, so I get to meet the amazing Paxton Holt after all of these years in the shadows."

I looked at him with anger. "Who the hell are you and what are you doing with Catherine?"

"Paxton, Paxton, Paxton." The man smiled with great deliberation. "Those answers will take longer then you have left to live. You will have read stories about me. You will have heard rumors about me, but I am the one the vampires revere."

"Judas?" Shock flooded through me. "It's not possible. You are a myth."

"Oh, Paxton," he sneered. "How disappointing. You cast doubt upon my presence and yet here I am. The first vampire."

"Then why have you hidden in the shadows for all these years? A vampire of your age and power could have taken the Covenant of Dark and controlled it instead of Vigo."

"Vigo was a child that did not have proper vision." Judas was contemptuous. "He fell in love with a witch but she was also a vampire. This was never meant to be his path. We fought a long and bloody battle. He assumed he had killed me. So I thought I would stay dead until the time was right. It took 1,500 years but here I am." Judas paced up and down on the stage as he spoke, with barely suppressed excitement. I knew he had been waiting a long time to tell me his story.

"Now I have an army at my disposal, those that have been born and those I have created. You have met one of my followers." He pointed to the hooded assassin. "He informed me that he has killed your friend. I would have loved to have seen that – in all its messy tragic glory." He shivered with delight.

I felt the beginnings of a dark rage billowing inside me. The room began to shake.

"I see you have some magic inside of you. You will be a perfect match for Ronen…Oh how rude I am, the one you call the hooded figure has gone by many names in his time, the reaper for one. But instead of telling you, why not let Ronen show you."

I felt myself swallow. It was a very theatrical experience but I knew that Judas was ultra-confident and there would be a reason for that. It was going to be very difficult to defeat them both.

"Now he never shows his face except before a kill," Judas informed me. "However, since you will soon be dead, I am sure he would love to show you his face." Judas laughed, "Also, let's make this even more fun." Judas pointed his finger at Gastin and he lurched helplessly from the floor, as his chain on the wall

PROPHECY

released. His body floated over to the stage and hovered in the air. "If you lose, you get to see him die."

"And when I win?"

Judas narrowed his eyes and looked at me strangely. "Then you are all free to go. You have my word."

I looked at Judas as he sat back on the throne. Gastin was still floating in midair as his hands unbound by chains were instead bound by magic. He was held in place and frozen into position but he could move his eyes and I could see his sudden fear, but there was something else too, I could sense it…disbelief. The hooded figure, Ronen, walked towards me, his posture and movement jaunty, his hood still in place.

"Don't trust them, Paxton," Catherine's voice rang out into the silent room.

Judas waved his hands, a quick flick of his wrists sending a surge of magic at Catherine, rendering her unconscious. I swallowed, I had to win, I had to free her and Gastin. I did not dare let a single thing distract me. I watched in silence as Ronen slipped the hood from his face. I took a step back, my knees buckling. "This is not possible," I breathed.

Judas chuckled. "Think of it this way, Paxton, it appears that God and the Devil have a sense of humor. Who'd have thought?" He leaned back in his throne. "But really, remember that the two of you are the last of the hunters. A secret fail-safe. A balancing act. Meaning that if one was good, there always had to be one who was pure evil. He is your dark shadow."

I looked up at Ronen, the dark hunter. He was the image of me. How was I to kill myself? How could I fight my physical equal?

"I can see you are shocked, Paxton. So let me give you more information. When the hunter was created, to keep the balance, one figure was created from both sides. You are the epitome of good." Judas made a face as if he were sick to his stomach. "Ronen was created to be the side for evil. It was all part of the balance, only today, it will favor our side."

I knew that today was the ultimate in battles. How many men could say they were truly fighting themselves? Gastin, Catherine, and the baby, they needed me. But more than that, the fate of mankind rested on my shoulders.

"Have you thought what happens if one of us dies? If we were created for balance, what does that do to the equilibrium of the planet?" I asked Judas.

Judas paused, contemplating for a moment, running his fingers through his long beard. He stood up suddenly, his mind occupied and I took the chance to throw the kill instrument at him, it spun at a deadly speed but he stopped it from completely impaling his chest.

The force of the impact had thrown Judas back into his throne. He sat hunched over, silent. For a moment, I felt my fear subsiding. Then a hollow, bitter laugh from Judas, who stood up with the kill instrument still buried in his chest. He reached down and grabbed it, pulling it out with great force. I heard the popping sound as it exited his body. It did not burn his hands either as it had done to so many other supernatural creatures.

PROPHECY

Ronen stood there motionless just waiting for his master's command. "You see, hunter, this instrument does not have the same effect on me as it does my other children. I cannot be killed that way. There is only one way to end me and that you will never know. Search your beloved Hunter's Journal. You will find nothing."

Without hesitation, Judas took the kill instrument and broke it in half. I felt my heart jolt. It felt like losing an appendage. It resumed a form of power in Judas' hands as he looked at both halves. He took one and threw it to me and the other to Ronen. The half he threw to me was red. It felt different in my hands, but I could feel that it still held some power. Ronen's half was black, and he bent down to pick it up. Now we each had a half of the deadliest weapon. I had no clue as to what the kill instrument would do to him or to me.

"Win and you and your friends go free. Lose and you are all mine forever to do with as I please." Judas stared into my eyes. "It's time."

I had no choice but to fight. I didn't know if he had any weak areas but I had to assume we would be evenly matched. I had to hold on to my anger, remember him as the killer of my friend.

"It is a shame that you must die," Ronen said. "I would have like to learn more from you. Knowledge is power, and we are two halves of the same mold."

I sensed his arm movement, moving as he lunged in. The sword and kill instrument were met with a solid defense and he was also able to land a glancing blow on my face. The cut healed quickly. It was nothing but a warning. My friends over the years had taught me so much about fighting; I knew I had to tap into their experiences and fighting styles rather than to just rely on my own natural instinct. I thought about Lars and all he had taught me. His bravery, loyalty, and his skill. I focused my mind and breathed deeply. I didn't want to face up to the loss of Lars yet, I just prayed I would have no one else to mourn.

* * *

Just outside of the front gates, Gloria and the remaining vampires and werewolves were pushing their way into the inner courtyard of the castle grounds. There, the battle raged on. Hayden fought with silver daggers deflecting bullet shots and using his quick movements to counteract the blows from his fellow supernatural brothers. Ethan on the other hand was still in full rage mode. Although embedded with arrowheads and riddled with bullets, he refused to slow down. His mission was set: destroy whatever got in his way. The others knew that it was best to stand back and to let him have his fun.

As Ethan powered his way through the mob, Gloria was able to watch him healing instantly. She had never seen anything quite like it. The bullets that had penetrated his skin were being pushed out by the healing of his flesh. As he killed, he also fed, grabbing food on the run, drinking their blood, consuming their energies and powers. He could also recall their memories. This fueled his desire even more. He fought a general, one of the more powerful vampires of the enemy crew. Amazed by Ethan's ability to continue irrespective of his injuries, he pulled out his sword and thrust it deeply into Ethan's chest. Ethan's body jerked under the sudden pressure. With blood gushing out, Ethan grabbed the general and pulled him closer, sending the sword ever deeper into his own body. Ethan continued to pull the general close. He finally bit down on the old vampire's neck and drank. He supped greedily until all the blood was gone from his body. As he consumed his blood, he consumed his memories too.

Ethan saw the vision of a man seated on a throne giving orders to kill a couple and their child. He also saw a strangely familiar hooded figure being sent to carry out this order. Ethan's rage reached a critical level. As he finished drinking the last drops of blood, he grabbed the lifeless body of the general, throwing him up into the air, and then ripped him in half. He pulled out his internal organs and threw them onto the floor. When he finished, he ground the organs to pulp.

* * *

Ronen's blows were powerful. I felt as if my body was being ripped in half. I hoped I was having a similar effect on him. We utilized a similar fighting style and had a definitive agility helping us to bend, weave, and roll our way out of trouble. I could not see this fight ending soon. I was worried though. I didn't want to reveal my best move but if I got injured, I wouldn't be able to defeat Judas. I saw my opportunity and jumped for Ronen, landing awkwardly as he disappeared. I ducked just in time as Ronen reappeared, swinging his sword where my neck had been. I was lucky that my head was still on my shoulders.

We repeated our martial arts dance over and over. Disappearing and reappearing just as the other spotted an opening. I landed a glancing blow, knocking Ronen back, taking a defensive stance. Judas appeared to be overjoyed by our display of skills.

"Bravo, bravo, you two make one unbeatable team. I just wish you could join us, Paxton; we would be able to execute my plan to the fullest with your combined powers."

"I would never join you. You have to have me killed to stop me coming for you," I spat at him.

He frowned with false regret. "Exactly why Ronen is going to kill you soon."

Judas walked towards us. "Lower your weapons – both of you."

Ronen and I looked at each other as we did so, waiting for a sudden aggressive move.

"Paxton, do you understand what this entire thing is about?" Judas asked.

I looked at him. "Your extreme power perhaps?"

"Power yes, but there is so much more." Judas walked around me not fearing my blade. "You understand I have been alive for over 2,000 years and I have lain low for all this time. I have created my children who have created an empire based on my legacy. It's time to take that back, it's my birthright to control."

I waited patiently for him to continue.

"So you see, Paxton, I planted a mole inside of Safe Haven and on the Covenant of Dark Council too. I had to find a way to break up the treaty to start a war between the two sides which meant that you would be

PROPHECY

distracted from my plans. I did it well too – don't you think?"

I gave him credit for that. It hadn't taken much to make the treaty crumble away like dust.

"The death of the Supreme Chancellor was always planned since the new Supreme Chancellor is completely under my control. Slowly I infiltrated the ranks on both sides."

"What about the insurgents, the Children of Judas?"

Judas laughed. "You like the name? I didn't even come up with it. It was all part of the plan to keep you off your guard and us off your radar. It also enabled us to infiltrate different parts of Safe Haven and the Dark Council. Paxton, you were the pawn used to create the final draw. Create war between the two sides. I had hoped you would be killed during the ambush along with your friends, but not all plans work out the way you want."

"The soldiers of Safe Haven are forcing their way into the castle even now," I said. "You can't fight them all."

"Yes," Judas said, "that is unfortunate; I will deal with them shortly. But you don't have to worry about your friends. I will kill them fast. In fact, I will give you that as a gift especially if you let Ronen kill you."

Ronen looked angry. "Master, no. I will destroy him on my own."

"Patience, Ronen, know your place and speak only when I say you can. Is that understood?"

I saw a flash of anger in Ronen's eyes and wondered if this could be the weakness I had been looking for. "What about Catherine and my unborn child?"

"Hmmm, well, I don't care about Catherine. Your child however is very interesting. As I regain my power and complete control of the vampire empire, we need to experiment on the child. If it survives, I will take the child in as my own."

My anger fired up and the room began to shake again. Yes, I thought, use this energy, focus it, and channel it. Use it against Ronen. I contained it, picturing a flick switch where I could access it at will.

"Tell me more," I said grimly.

"Paxton, I can't share everything with you, that would not be good." Judas mocked me as if I were some naughty child overstepping the mark.

"Why not? You said it yourself that Ronen will end me. He is just as powerful as I am and has magic that I have never seen, what are you worried about?"

Judas considered this point and acquiesced. "Very well. There are several things currently that restrain vampires and yet humans take full advantage of."

"The sun," I said slowly.

"Yes, Paxton. Your child may well hold the key to walking in the sun and perhaps to our never-ending hunger for blood. If vampires did not need to feed just on blood or to walk only at night, we wouldn't need to preserve humans at all. We could stop being their savior; convert 100 million of them into vampires and control this world permanently."

PROPHECY

No wonder Judas was both revered and feared. He was quite mad. He had waited all this time using the prophecy to fuel this world domination plan.

"Can you imagine it? Hell on earth. I would become a god. Ironic really." He smirked.

He continued, "My witches have told me that your child may possess extraordinary abilities and the blood may give us what we need. So do you see why your child is so important to us? I just wish you could understand that. I would give you power and control if you joined me. You could sit beside me with Catherine and your child and rule them all. You still have one last chance. You need to decide, and quickly or Ronen will be by my side living the dream that could be for you."

"Never."

Ronen surged forward. His speed was frightening and I rolled out of the way.

"You are a fool, Ronen. You follow Judas and yet he just offered me power over you. Think about it. He thinks so little of you."

I slashed at his face with my sword but he flipped backwards, throwing a dagger at me. I moved just in time and the dagger embedded in the wall behind me. I dived over the top of him, slicing with my sword in midair. His skin parted like butter and blood splattered across the room. As I landed, I flipped to the side and around, using my sword with one hand, slashing his legs and then up from the spine to the neck. He was bleeding but healing fast. He slammed his sword into the ground and I did the same. Utilizing the power of the universe we called the energy to us and then projected it at each other. Our forces were evenly met. There were no lightning bolts or amazing colors, just a fuzzy, shimmering, golden light that connected us both.

I had been hit by this before. It was the reason Lars had died. I conjured up all the power by using my love for my family and my memories. It was these memories that brought about an untapped power. I felt it grow from the bowels of my gut. It was as if all those that had died were inside of me. I could feel Vladimir, my mother, my father, Clay, Nina, and even Lars. They were my strength. I allowed this acknowledgement to wash over me, bringing up this power and igniting it from my hands, sending a shock wave towards Ronen, and he flew backwards hitting the wall, the front of his body burning. I watch his body judder.

Suddenly, I felt strong. I was not alone, I felt different. There was no fear of death. My power came from all those who had been a part of my life. Their spirits, alive and dead, seemed to give me strength. I grabbed the half of the kill instrument and my sword. As I ran, I engaged all the powers, my determination, and my resolve. My revenge was for Lars and all that had died for this cause. Their deaths were not pointless. They died in a belief of a better world and a spiritual afterlife. Ronen, still groggy, came at me with the same weapons. We met in the middle of the room and an echo of our violent encounter reverberated through the castle and beyond. It was blade against blade and kill instrument against kill instrument.

As steel met steel, smoke and sparks were emitted from the weapons. Ronen spotted an opportunity, sneaking in with a dangerous attack and a spell that would disarm

PROPHECY

me. The spell worked partially, but it only dislodged the kill instrument, which landed near Gastin's feet as he hovered midair watching helplessly. I attacked back, with a slash to Ronen's thigh and another to his wrist, which dislodged his kill instrument. He healed pretty quickly again but I could see wavering doubt in his eyes.

From the corner of my eye, I saw a soldier from the castle guards approach Judas and advise that the Covenant of Light had broken through their defenses. It was just a matter of time before they infiltrated the core part of the castle. I sensed Judas' sudden surge of fear. The battle was not as clear-cut as he had envisaged. That fueled my strength yet more.

As Judas made his way to the breached wall, he took the form that the Devil had given him. He was enormous and terrifying and twice the size of any vampire. He was also the strongest. The curse that God had placed upon vampires and werewolves extended out to all of his bloodline. Judas however was immune to almost all the ills that affected his children. In this form, he walked to the great walls of his inner sanctum. There his guards readied themselves for battle. Judas knew his objective and that was to kill Gloria at all cost. He would worry about the rest afterwards.

With the gates to his inner sanctum open, the soldiers set up a barrier against the oncoming vampires and werewolves. Gloria was in the crowd. Judas saw her as she was in full form. She was a large werewolf and very powerful. As werewolves and vampires aged, they become stronger, and for all that had passed through the gates of Safe Haven, none had matched her strength.

Judas ran forward, his goal in sight. He tossed soldiers of the Covenant of Light from side to side, ripping them in half as he surged forward, drinking their blood. When he saw his opportunity to take Gloria, he relished the moment ahead when she would meet her death. As he moved forward, he was met by a mighty force that threw him against the castle wall. Judas hit the wall, his body embedded within the stonework while the walls shook, stonework tumbling down on top of him.

Judas struggled to free himself. He was injured but not fatally. With a final surge of energy, he pulled himself free and stood before Ethan. He sniffed the air, and viewed Ethan's form from side to side. There was a familiarity. Something tugged at his memory banks.

Ethan had learned that the hooded figure Ronen had been sent to kill his family and to capture him. Since the hooded figure worked for Judas, Ethan had decided that Judas would feel his vengeance. Ethan saw Judas prepare to charge at him, relying on his power, and he anticipated his move. Ethan charged at him and their joint force was so powerful that it sent many of the smaller werewolves falling to their deaths on the rocks below.

Judas knew that this young vampire could not possibly overpower him. He was over 2,000 years old and the most powerful of all vampires. Ethan didn't see this, nor was he intimated by Judas. They were the same size but Ethan kept pushing, filled with the memories of his parents' untimely death. The sheer power of Ethan splintered the ground, causing the foundations beneath Judas to sink and he dropped down, shocked. He clung to the crumbling foundations, calling for his guards to

PROPHECY

attack Ethan. As they responded, Ethan brushed them aside like ants but it gave Judas the seconds needed for him to regain his position and to overpower Ethan, throwing him against the castle wall. He jumped over the battling army, landing on top of Ethan, throwing punch after punch at his face. At first it appeared as if Judas had Ethan defeated and as the blood flowed from Ethan's monstrous face, battered, bloody but still resilient, he looked up and smiled at Judas.

In sheer anger, Judas kept punching and his power grew every time his fist connected. Withdrawing into himself, Ethan searched for and felt a strength that was greater than had already been displayed. He felt no pain, just the pleasure of revenge to come, he could taste the moment where he would snap Judas into pieces. Ethan's body became shielded, his muscles hardened like stone.

Ethan deflected the next blow and pushed his hand into Judas' chest cavity. His hand surged through skin that was tougher than any vampire's and snapped bone that was akin to the strongest steel. He reached the heart and squeezed, harder and harder. Judas had never been handled as such. He had never truly lost a battle or been at a point where his death was a possibility.

Judas roared for assistance, his pain alerting all. As the soldiers rushed towards them, they left Gloria and Hayden to enter the main hall. With the onslaught of the other vampires, Ethan was forced to let go. Judas fell back; his heart pumping hard, writhing in agony, blood spurting from the hole in his chest. He used all his energy to heal, letting the power surge through his body. He needed help and grabbed one of the vampire soldiers, drinking his blood, draining him dry. He discarded the body, throwing it aside. He staggered away, hearing Ethan's angry threats ringing out.

"You can't run forever! I will find you and I will kill you, do you hear me? Your fate is sealed. I am your reaper and I will find you and I will collect!"

* * *

Inside, Gloria scented the air to try to find Catherine and Paxton. She could sense someone else as well. "Gastin?" She knew they had to be somewhere close, she could sense fear and pain. But where were they? With the help of Hayden, she started down the great hall looking for their friends.

* * *

I felt rather than saw Judas return. My heart sank. I had so wanted to have finished Ronen off before he had returned. I could feel my disappointment ebbing my strength away. Ronen, on the other hand, seemed to be getting stronger. I saw the fire of victory start to burn in his eyes. I suddenly felt Catherine's distress and flipped over Ronen's head to see what was happening.

Judas had grabbed Catherine, who was growing visibly weaker. She was still in her magical shackles and helpless. Judas licked her face, leaving wet slime across her cheek. Catherine had no strength to fight back, she needed blood. He squeezed her thigh, moving his hands up higher. Judas smiled, his hands touching her extended stomach. The baby was growing fast and the unborn child seemed to flinch under his touch.

"I think I will keep her around as a pet, sort of a plaything." He looked at me. "But, we are family...so

PROPHECY

maybe I only play and punish her a little." He trailed his fingers down her body, over the curve of her breast and onto her stomach, pushing hard until she screamed.

"I will take the child in and if my experiments do not work, I will just kill the child when asleep. A knife to the throat maybe," Judas taunted me.

He licked Catherine's face again, his tongue licking her lips and then down over her throat. She was almost fainting. Once again, he pressed on her stomach bringing her back from her near unconscious state and she screamed, unable to protect herself or the baby.

My anger knew no bounds. I pushed Ronen back and combined magic with my mastery of the sword. He anticipated well and returned the spell until it cancelled itself out. The power was dead even. Neither of us had the advantage. I called for the kill instrument but Judas, having crept away from Catherine, stepped on it.

I tuned into all those who had gone before me and found a sudden surge of power. I was stronger and faster than I could ever remember. I started to strike at Ronen, my speed catching him unawares, slashing his leg and then his shoulder. He fought back, defending the blows, but I had utilized the power of the former hunters. Ronen crumbled under the sheer force of my blows. The last swing of my sword shattered Ronen's.

"It's over, Ronen. It ends now," I said triumphantly.

Just as I embraced victory, I felt the sharp end of the kill machine enter my back, tearing me open. I heard Catherine scream in fear. The pain was excruciating. I saw Ronen roll to the side, grabbing the other half of the kill instrument and plunging it deep into my chest. I staggered back, pain tearing through my body. As I turned, I saw Gastin, his face expressionless, just watching. How had he become free?

"Why?" I asked as I staggered, my legs weak, pain surging through me.

"I did it for Gloria. Your kind should have never touched her with your filthy human hands. She belongs to me." His voice was contemptuous. The traitor in our midst had finally spoken.

I looked at Catherine in disbelief as a tear ran down her face.

"I'm sorry," I whispered to her. I knew her tears were blinding her. It was the end of us all. I tried to pull the kill instrument out of my body but couldn't. I dropped to my knees, the room spinning, and my insides dissolving. "I love you," I said and then fell face down, my eyes still open, my heart beating – just.

Judas ordered his soldiers to grab Catherine and Ronen.

Gastin looked at Judas and said, "What about me, my Lord?"

"There will be questions, many questions about you. So let them be true."

"What questions, my Lord?"

Judas smiled at Gastin. "About your death, of course."

Before Gastin could react, Judas pulled out his sword and cut Gastin's head from his body. He watched the head roll across the ground until it eventually came to rest, rocking as if in disbelief. He waited until the body had folded and collapsed, and then turned to follow the

PROPHECY

others. Ronen was helped out by several soldiers and although his injuries were severe, he would be able to heal. Judas also ordered that they take the body of Paxton and an ever weak Catherine from the castle. They used secret passageways that led to a helicopter on the roof.

In less than a minute, Ethan smashed through the bolted doors to the banqueting hall. In the middle of the floor Gastin lay in two pieces. Gloria ran over, swallowing hard. It was over. Her life would never be the same again with the loss of two of her greatest friends. She saw the sword owned by Lars and took it with her, sensing that Paxton and Catherine had been here only recently. She pushed the death of her dear friend Gastin to one side, she would grieve in her own time but for now, she still had a battle on her hands.

As they searched the myriad of tunnels, Gloria's sharp ears heard the sound of a helicopter approaching and they ran out of the castle and up onto the hill which was the highest point. Gloria, Hayden, and Ethan stood silently with a handful of soldiers that had survived the ferocity of the battle. They watched as the helicopter flew away, a sense of anger and hopeless frustration sweeping over them. Gloria could feel death and decay all around her. Something was very wrong, a sick premonition but she couldn't pinpoint the feeling. She said a silent prayer that Paxton and Catherine would be safe.

In the chopper, Ronen, Judas, and several of the armed guards sat near Paxton's prone body. The kill instruments were still firmly in his body.

Judas barked orders at the pilot. "Stay the course. I would like to be at my families' cemetery as quickly as possible." He sat back in his seat, a faint smile hovering around his lips. A satisfying day. The death of Paxton Holt and the kidnap of Catherine. Soon he would have that child out of her and would be able to make many tests on its blood. Soon, the planet would belong to the vampires and he would be the master of all.

Time ticked by. Catherine watched for any movement from Paxton but there was none. She couldn't believe it. He really was dead.

The pilot signaled that they were approaching their destination. Catherine remained in the helicopter, crying softly as they took Paxton's body away. She watched them carry him towards the great tomb. With its thickened walls and the pungent smell of death and decay, Judas felt it was a fitting place for Paxton Holt. He had been a true hunter and now here was his resting place for all time. Two guards carried the body into the tomb and placed him inside a giant marble sarcophagus.

"I give this resting place to a worthy adversary," Judas stated and nodded towards Paxton.

Ronen leaned in and closed Paxton's unstaring eyes and then watched as the two guards struggled with the marble top, sliding it back into place.

"It is time that the dark rise up from the night and look into the sun. Soon, we will be free from the chains of dependency and we will thrive under the summer sun," Judas chanted as he watched them seal Paxton into the sarcophagus.

PROPHECY

They exited the tomb and Ronen sealed it. He used all his remaining energy to power his incantation. Nothing could enter or leave this tomb. It was sealed with the strongest magic he knew.

Back in the helicopter, the final stages of discussions were taking place. The plan was to take over the council, destroy any soldiers left and to kill Gloria of Safe Haven. Judas was savoring that moment the most.

"Soon we will have all the power that we need. The world is changing and with the coming of this child we will have a world filled with vampires." Judas looked at Catherine.

"Feel honored, Catherine. You are finally doing something worthy with your life."

"I won't let you hurt my child," she told him, hatred blazing from her eyes.

Judas smiled. "My dear, you have no say in the matter. Be thankful that your baby needs you at the moment, otherwise you would be dead already."

Catherine could only watch through the helicopter as she looked past Judas and the others towards the tomb. "Paxton, please don't be dead. Please." She sent her energy and love up into the ethers, begging the universe to honor and save Paxton. Tears rolled down her cheeks, how could she live without him? She watched helplessly as the tomb faded into the distance as the helicopter lifted up and they traveled over the rugged scenery dropping away below.

Her eyes caught sight of a crow, flying past the window, its glossy black wings flapping against the wind. It was strange to see one up so high but she soon lost sight of it and the memory faded from her mind as she slipped into melancholy. She had no energy left to fight, no will to survive. Nothing left to live for.

The crow dipped down circling around the cemetery, eventually landing on a perch above the tomb that held Paxton. There, at the top of the tomb, a small opening allowed light into the darkness below. It landed, pecking at the thickened glass, watching the marble below. It continued to tap, harder and harder onto the glass. Day passed to night and the crow kept a vigil. Tapping the glass as the light from the moon shone through at just the right angle. The silver beam shone onto the body of Paxton Holt, lying in death's grip, in his resting place for eternity. As the hours passed and the moonlight continued to shine down on him, the crow tilted its head as if listening and watching, a slight movement, a twitch of fingers, a faint breath emitted from his mouth.

Above him, the crow tapped as if with a welcome and an acknowledgement of life as Paxton Holt let out a strangled cry. "Catherine!"

The battle wasn't over yet!

Appendix

*****

Covenant of Light:

Gloria (b. 1468 AD) – leader of the Covenant of Light. She is a pureblood werewolf and over 500 years old. She formed the separation of factions between good and evil with Abraham the hunter. They erected a fortress call Safe Haven in a remote part of Canada. Safe Haven takes in supernatural creatures that denounce evil and follow the light.

Gastin (b. 1621 AD) – a powerful werewolf, second in command of Gloria's werewolf army and mayor of their isolated town in Colorado, population 200. Gastin was one of the Band of Six that helped to bring Paxton Holt to Safe Haven for training.

Paxton Holt (b. 1986 AD) – the eleventh in a line of hunters that protect mankind from evil supernatural creatures. The mantle of hunter was passed to him from Vladimir, who died while trying to protect him. He also received a powerful weapon called the kill instrument. Paxton has been the hunter for over 200 years and is virtually immortal. A hunter only dies if his head is taken or if another hunter is chosen while he is still alive.

Catherine (b. Unknown) – daughter of Olivia and Vigo, a pureblood vampire and direct descendant of Judas, the very first vampire. She is one of only three vampires who have ever been able to walk during daylight. She falls in love with Paxton Holt before he becomes a hunter. Her father opposes their love because hunters are the enemy.

Hayden (b. 1586 AD) – a very old werewolf with blood-red hair. He has served both sides, but chose the side of the light after Abraham saved him in the battle of New Orleans. He is known for his understanding of schematics for tunnels and ability to track. He was the main guide in leading Paxton the hunter to Gloria and Safe Haven.

Lars (b. 1114 AD) – one of the most feared sword fighters in the world. He helped the Covenant of Dark defeat the hunter William Stanton. Later Lars joined the Covenant of Light to help his brother Virgil avenge their father's death at the hands of Vigo. Lars joined the Band of Six to lead Paxton Holt to Gloria at Safe Haven to be trained.

Virgil (b. 920 AD) – a second-generation pureblood vampire. His father Desman was second in command to Vigo until Desman fought and eventually lost to Vigo. Virgil is devastated by this and joins with Gloria and Abraham to form the Covenant of Light. They fight for the preservation of all that is good.

Clay (b. 1562 AD – d. 2003 AD) – a werewolf that worked with Gloria and the Covenant of Light. He was sent by Gloria to track Vladimir after Abraham's death. Clay got caught in the midst of several alphas and Vladimir came to his rescue. Vladimir joined the Covenant of Light and Clay fought by his side up to Vladimir's death. He then befriended the new hunter Paxton Holt and sacrificed his life to save Paxton.

PROPHECY

Nina (b. 1792 AD – d. 2025) – a human from a line of witches that dates back 15 generations. She spent most of her time in New Orleans where magic is the strongest. She could change her form to a black panther, read minds, and communicate through thought. In 1920 Nina was saved by Vladimir and Gloria from a group of powerful vampires and joined the Covenant of Light. She later became one of the Band of Six.

Safe Haven – A fortress hidden in a remote part of Canada. It is a refuge for the Covenant of Light. An enchantment cloaks it and keeps enemies out. It's said that the enchantment can tell if a person seeking Safe Haven has good intentions. If they do, it will permit them to pass inside. Another way to pass is if invited by a senior member of Safe Haven. More than 200 werewolves and vampires are estimated to reside there.

Covenant of Dark:

PHLC (Preservation of Human Life Corporation) – A mega-company that grew from businesses run and owned by the Dark Covenant in many different industries: technology, film (Darkside Pictures), science (cryogenics), and pharmaceuticals, to name a few. By the end of World War III (2045-2067), countries had stopped making alliances and trading with each other, and the world's population had dipped from 7 billion to 3.5 billion. The PHLC was then allowed to form a monopoly on trade for two reasons. The first was that there were no more regulatory agencies, and the second was that vampire doctors had found a way to create medication from vampire DNA that did not change a human to a vampire but instead cured many diseases, sped up recovery time, and slowed the aging process.

The vampires didn't do this to save humanity, but to increase their business and keep their food supply from dwindling away.

Supreme Chancellor Joakim Fredrik (b. 625 AD) – a powerful pureblood vampire. He was born in Sweden to two vampire parents. He was elected Supreme Chancellor after the previous one was killed by William Stanton in 1598 AD. He was considered by many of his peers in the Dark Covenant to be a vampire capitalist. He was also one of the driving forces to create the treaty between the Covenants of Dark and Light.

Assistant Chancellor Baldassare Vega (b. 1346 AD) – the first Italian pureblood appointed to the level of Assistant Chancellor in the council's 1,500-year history. His father was a pureblood, but his mother was turned; she was a half-breed. He moved up the ranks quickly. Vigo saw his love for his kind and hatred for other supernatural creatures as a sign of loyalty. This led Vigo to appoint him to his post in 1867 AD.

Priscilla Rehborn (b.1635 AD) – the highest-ranking female on the council. She was born in Germany to two pureblood parents. She has over 600 years of war and lust wrapped up in her petite frame. She supports no cause that does not directly benefit her. A tremendous warrior, she has had several run-ins with hunters and lived to tell the story.

Josiah Black (b. 867 AD) – from Portugal, he is the longest-serving member on the council, having served for over 1,100 years. He is dedicated to the old ways. He believes that one day Judas will come back and deliver them from what is going on in the world. He is believed to have coined the name "The Children of

PROPHECY

Judas" for the cult that supports the old ways and tries to stop anyone that does not follow the path set for them by Judas.

General Lark (b. 763 AD) – one of Vigo's top three soldiers. After Vigo's death and the treaty between the Covenant of Light and Dark, General Lark went underground. He started to gather followers to continue Vigo's cause. An unidentified benefactor to help fund his war approached him. He is the main commander of the Children of Judas.

Captain Rocco Bernard (b. 1734 AD) – one of two known werewolf-vampire hybrids and captain of the Supreme Chancellor's personal guard. In his normal form he is about 6 foot tall; as a werewolf he is close to 10 feet tall. He can be distinguished from other werewolves by his distinctive all-white coat. As a hybrid he is immune to silver. Also, his vital organs in his rib cage are encased in hard bone. This shell requires tremendous force to break it. A stake through the heart or beheading will kill him.

Redfire (b. 1612 AD) – neither werewolf nor vampire, but one of the very few working warlocks. He was born in the 1600s into a very powerful tribe of female witches who trained him. To feed his insatiable desire for power, he killed the witches one by one, eating their hearts and burning their bodies – inhaling their essence as they burned. The few who escaped named him Redfire. He is also the best tracker the Covenant of Dark has ever had.

Brock (b. 2052 AD) – a werewolf turned in his twenties. He is a unique half-breed. He was born with a deformity that caused his bones to be very thick and dense. When he was bitten and turned, the genetic mutation simply fixed the abnormalities and even thickened and strengthened his structure. He is hard to kill because he has twice the thickness and density of a pureblood's bones.

Liam Vega (b. 1812 AD) – son of Assistant Chancellor Baldassare Vega. The exact circumstances of his birth are unknown. What is known is that he is a pureblood vampire and one of the greatest sword fighters in the world. He is also a skilled assassin that can make any object into an instrument to kill.

Historical Figures:

William Stanton (b. 1505 AD – d. 1608 AD) – the eighth hunter out of the 11 that have held that title. He was killed in 1608 in England while fighting off a horde of vampires. Lars, the youngest son of Desman, finally defeated him. The sword battle lasted hours. He is documented as killing over 18 vampires and werewolves until Lars beheaded him. The legend of William Stanton is documented in the Hunters' Journal.

Abraham (b. 1686 AD – d. 1861 AD) – number nine in the line of hunters. Abraham was over 175 years old when he died at the church where Vladimir was a pastor. Abraham, a blacksmith, never had a family and was truly involved in his work and God.

Desman (b. 542 AD – d. 1608 AD) – the father of Virgil and Lars. He also was the second in command on the Vampire Council. He saw that Vigo was taking human massacres too far and tried to get the council to stop him. Vigo ousted Desman, banished him, and dishonored anyone within his family. Desman later

PROPHECY

fought Vigo with help from Abraham, a powerful hunter, but lost his life in the process.

Vladimir (b. 1802 AD – d. 2003 AD) – one of the most powerful hunters. He killed over 3,000 vampires and werewolves. He was a pastor before becoming a hunter. His adopted family was killed by Vigo, and he vowed to destroy Vigo. Vladimir never killed Vigo, but did kill his oldest son Henley and Voss, his most trusted ally.

Vigo (b. over 1,800 years ago-d. 2035) – Lord of the Vampires and oldest after Judas. He was the only child of Judas the first vampire and Lyka his sister the first werewolf. He had three children, Henley, John, and Catherine. Only Catherine survives. Abraham and Vladimir killed Henley. John disappeared in the 1300s and is presumed dead.

Significant Human:

Deloris Harris (b. 1939 AD) – an American woman of African descent. She falls in love with John, a man whose family is from Germany, but he dies early on in their marriage. Their daughter gives birth to a son, but dies on the way home from the hospital. Deloris knows more than she is telling her grandson Paxton about his destiny. Deloris is forever filled with guilt, because she believes she never did all she could to save her daughter.

Miscellaneous:

The Hunters' Journal – a journal that was given to Thomas at the same time the kill instrument was. It is a way for the hunters to document their history as well as anything they have learned about enemies, secret hideouts, and fighting styles. Much of it has been recorded in the moments just before a hunter's death. No one but a hunter or someone who is pure of heart can see the words, and all hunters are able to understand all that is written, whatever their native language. The journal cannot be destroyed by anything on earth. When a hunter dies or a new one is chosen, the kill instrument and the journal summon the new hunter to where they both are hidden or were last seen.

The Kill Instrument – the weapon created by God to help protect the hunter from other supernatural beings. The kill instrument assumes the form of a spike of solid oak for a vampire or solid silver for a werewolf. It appears to ordinary people as a broken piece of wood, but this is camouflage. It was created from wood from the very cross that Jesus died on. No one but a hunter can hold it and a hunter cannot be killed by it.

Rule of Royalty – Vigo, the oldest and most powerful of all the vampires, created the Rule of Royalty. Any direct descendant of Judas is considered royal and a pureblood. This rule was created to purify the race, because born vampires possess more power than someone that was turned. This new covenant became known as the Covenant of Dark. Through this Vigo created the Vampire Council. Purebloods would rule over the half-breeds, creating two classes.

Vampire Children – it takes 100 years for them to be considered full-grown. Also, a child born to a full-blood vampire and a half-blood vampire is considered a pureblood. Unlike other vampires that are changed, born vampires still possess their souls; they have to kill an innocent to relinquish their soul. In doing so they

PROPHECY

increase all their physical attributes like strength, speed, durability, etc.

The Originals:

Judas – one of the original twelve apostles of Jesus Christ. He betrayed Jesus out of anger and in guilt made a deal with the devil to become immortal. This tradeoff led to Judas becoming the first vampire. (See Story of Thomas, next page.)

Lyka – the sister of Judas who becomes the first werewolf. She produced a child, Vigo, with her brother Judas. Because she convinced her brother to betray Jesus for 30 silver pieces, Jesus puts two curses on her and any that come after. No one knows for sure if Lyka is still alive or just a myth. (See Story of Thomas, next page.)

The Story of Thomas: The Origin of the Hunters:

Thomas, one of the original 12 apostles of Jesus Christ and the very first hunter, tells the first story in the great journal of the hunters. He tells of the creation of the hunter: that it was an honor and a curse. It all began after the death of Jesus Christ. Upon the crucifixion of Jesus, the devil rose from below and possessed a rat that watched Jesus as he was hoisted on the cross. The devil thought this was his opportunity to rise up from hell to take over mankind, but to the devil's dismay just the opposite happened.

This sacrifice was spurred on by one of Jesus' own apostles, Judas, who betrayed the heart of Jesus. The devil thought that with Jesus' death humankind would lose faith and embrace the devil's desires. However, the moment that Jesus' life left him he had forgiven all that were against him and in doing so took the sins of all.

Jesus' sacrifice wounded the devil so much that it caused a crack in his prison of hell. This crack was wide enough for souls to escape and be judged by God himself with an opportunity to ascend to the gates of heaven.

The devil sensed he had one last chance to strike before being cast to hell forever. He took the form of Paul the apostle, the one who denied he knew Jesus but also was the most influential apostle of the twelve. The devil as Paul offered Judas a cup of wine that if he accepted he would be able to live forever by giving himself to the devil. Judas, still reeling in shame over what he had done, had planned to take his own life, but the devil was much too clever. He said that in the wake of the death of Jesus a great plague would come, wiping out all that is alive, and those who had given themselves to Jesus would be saved whereas Judas himself would be swallowed whole into the abyss.

Judas, seeing that Paul was telling him this, drank the wine to stave off death and to live forever. The devil then revealed himself to Judas who tried to recant his deal, but it was too late. The devil told him that with eternal life he would be strong and would have women, power, and riches. Judas conceded to the devil, who told him that as he lived on earth his soul would belong in hell. The devil also told him that if he could convince others of eternal life, the very life that God had taken from Adam and Eve, they too could live forever, but they had to accept the devil's deal as he had.

PROPHECY

The devil explained that since sin was free from the body, the way Judas would eat was by the blood of others. This would give him strength. The devil also told him to work fast since the plague was coming and more soldiers for the war against good were needed. Judas wasted no time; within a week he had over 100 men and women like him. These souls fed the devil and corrupted those who were without sin.

At the same time Jesus' body was laid to rest, until his resurrection, God willed him to meet with the devil who showed his form as a fox in a tree. Yes, Jesus, the devil said to him. Jesus said, I know what you have done. And because of this I banish all those that lust for blood to only live in the shadows, thus the light would never cover their skin like a silk sheet. It would cause great pain. Also, the heart, the only piece of their humanity, would be their undoing if it were ever forcefully shut by wood from a great tree, splintering the very blood that flowed through it. Jesus waved his hand and all the undead could be heard screaming in pain as they stood in the light searching for cover.

The devil didn't back down as the following day came and in the form of a man of prestige he approached the sister of Judas, the very person that caused the entire betrayal. It was prior to the last supper that Judas had come to the city to visit his sister and purchase wine and bread. With him he carried his fortune, 30 silver pieces. When he arrived at her house the weather outside chanced to a stormy mix. Judas was forced to stay. While he was there she tried to convince him against following the "false prophet" and turn Jesus in. She told him that just for telling the guards where Jesus was, a man would receive 30 silver pieces. Judas replied, but my wealth is already with me and in my faith of Jesus Christ. Judas' sister knew her brother was weak. She waited until he fell asleep and took his wealth, hiding it. When he awoke the next day, she cried wolf. She told him several men in white robes, looking for him, took his money. Judas was so filled with rage that he betrayed Jesus.

The devil was feeling an opportunity to slither his way to another deal. He approached Judas' sister. Wow, he said, what beauty, have I seen you before? Can I ask your name? You may, she said, my name is Lyka. What a pretty name, the devil said. The devil twisted his way to her heart and to the very thing that drove her, her "beauty." The devil told her that he had the ability to grant her a wish, filling her with amazement. The devil told her that she could make her wish and what she was inside would stay as it was on the outside, and she would have eternal life – but her soul would be his. Lyka did not think through her decision due to the blinding light of the idea of beauty everlasting. As her wish was completed her inner "beauty" transformed her physical form into a wolf. She became the wolf in sheep's clothing. This form she would keep for eternity. One bite from her lips or a scratch from her claws would lead others to the same fate. If they killed a human their souls would be condemned to hell.

The devil rejoiced at another sacrifice and more souls to come. Yet again God willed the devil and Jesus to meet on neutral grounds. Jesus with the word of God knew what the devil had done and again made a decree. Lyka and those like her would have the ability to have human form during the day. This form would separate the human from the wolf. If the human chose God and put

PROPHECY

his or her faith into Jesus he or she would be saved regardless of what the wolf did at night. They would be called werewolves. Due to the sin of Lyka, silver would be their undoing, either driven through the heart or enough to fill the body, which would cause it to fade away. If the human were good, the soul would go to heaven; if not, the human would go with the wolf to hell. The devil was now so enraged by what God had done that he went for Jesus. A light shined out, sending the devil running away. It was done. Jesus prayed to his Father who told him to bless a book of parchment and to take a piece of the very cross that held his body to fashion a weapon that could take the form of either a piece of wood for the blood drinker and or a piece of silver for the wolf. By the word of God, Jesus was told to choose someone to stop these atrocities before they consumed too many free souls. Jesus chose Thomas. After Jesus' resurrection, the New Testament talks about Thomas going to India to spread the word, but what it does not state, that it also was to bring judgment on the devil's children. Thus Thomas, one of the 12 apostles, became the first hunter and began his adventure in the name of Jesus Christ.

The Next Book From the Ashes
Prologue
*****

The light is very bright, it blinds me. I can't help think that I am dead. I close my eyes long enough to shield them from the sun. When I open them the bright burning light is gone. It is only daytime. The place I stand is no place I had been or seen in hundreds of years. It's like an untouched place. From the look of it, I am in a tropical forest. Not one I would see in Brazil or in the Congo of Africa but one that I had seen in movies as a child.

Well, there is no wasting time, but to walk. My mind tries to picture the moment right before Gastin pushed half of the kill instrument through my chest. This stirs up a burning feeling where the point entered in through my skin. As I lift up my shirt there is no scar. Nothing. You would believe that I made it all up. This feeling of déjà vu came over me as I walk. I can hear something and see another light as I come through the forest.

What I see surprises me. It's the beach. There is sand on either side of me. From the left I can see a cliff that has a giant statue of a soldier. Something from ancient times like Roman or even older. On the other side another cliff is the identical soldier. Maybe it's not a

PROPHECY

soldier, maybe it's a statue of a god. This entire place is confusing. As I look straight out from the beach I see endless ocean. Then I catch something strange that I didn't see before. It's the heat from two suns in the sky. Where am I truly?

My gazing at this phenomenon is interrupted by a voice. It seems to be coming from down the beach. Just 100 feet a way I see what looks like a woman walking back into the forest heading for the cliff where the giant stone figure stands. I yell out. "Hello, can you hear me? So you see me. Where are we, what is this place?" I run towards her as she disappears into the forest.

Once through the dense trees I see nothing, no woman. Could I have imagined her? She couldn't have disappeared that fast. Then I notice something that makes me believe I was not imagining it. On a branch leading up the cliff was a shawl.

As I bring it to my nose I notice it looks as if it had been there for ages but the smell on it is not of rain or wear of nature but of a person, a woman. I have no choice but to make my way up the cliff along the path. I have no clue what I will find at the top.

About The Author

*****

Eric M. Haberern is an author who currently resides in East Hartford, CT. He began writing at an early age. Writing has always been his passion. It wasn't until later in life that he was motivated to publish his first book, "Last Breath before Death." Since then Eric has worked on several additional projects and is looking forward to closing out the series with "From the Ashes."

For more information about this book or any possible follow-ups to this book, please tweet him @Eric Haberern or email him at erichaberern@gmail.com.

Made in the USA
Lexington, KY
24 April 2014